HAUNTED HAMBURGER HOUSE

FRANK J. EDLER

D & T
PUBLISHING

To Nick and Katrina for making me skeptical and to John and Chris for making me believe.

1

THIS PLACE IS NOT HAUNTED.

This place is not haunted.

This place is not haunted.

Addison Wilson repeated the phrase over and over in her head as she turned the key that locked the door to Hamburger House. This was now ritual whenever she attempted entry into the property. When she got into commercial reality, the last thing she expected to encounter was creepy vibes from an old hamburger joint.

She took a deep breath and let it escape her lungs like a breeze through a dark cave, "This place is not haunted," she said aloud before pulling the door open.

She entered Hamburger House and was greeted with a smell that was closer to an old barn than an abandoned fast-food restaurant. She took a step inside and looked around. The door clicked shut behind her and she jumped. It wasn't that dark inside, there were plenty of glass windows that surrounded the seating area. Tables and booths were covered with dusty tarps. The desert outside found its way in over the years, marching closer and closer to reclaiming this building to the badlands outside.

Addison never understood how anyone could have run a hamburger restaurant out here in the middle of nowhere. But Hamburger House sat off popular American highway Route 66 and saw lots of business in its heyday. The building was situated a quarter-mile off the old highway, a road traveled heavily by folks going west to visit Arizona, Nevada, and then onto California. When the meandering roadway was bypassed by Interstate 40, traffic and the associated business along the famed Route 66 vanished like a ghost.

Addison had tried, in vain, to appeal to locals interested in starting up their own business to consider Hamburger House. The place was still usable. Sure, you'd want to replace the grills, fryolators, and heating bins but for the most part, you could scrub the place down and get to work in no time.

She'd even tried to sell the lot that Hamburger House sat upon so that a potential buyer could knock the restaurant down and build to their needs. But nobody wanted to take on the added cost of demolishing a building and starting from scratch on a plot of land that didn't have much traffic.

All of that was beside the point. She couldn't get any buyers for this property because weird shit kept happening anytime she showed it to potential clients. Today, she was meeting with prospective buyers. She showed up early to feel the place out.

"Hello?"

She listened for an answer. None came.

She stepped to the front counter. There were three cash registers spread along its length, covered with more dusted tarps.

"I'm just going to show the place to some interested clients," Addison said to the restaurant, "They seem nice. They're an older couple. Retirees. They'd love to spend their golden years bringing this place back to life."

Addison felt stupid talking out loud to nobody at all. She also felt like she needed to calm the restaurant so that it wouldn't act up when the clients arrived.

She wanted to speak her mantra again to reassure herself but held back, not wanting to upset the restaurant if it was haunted after all.

On previous showings of Hamburger House, Addison encountered many strange sounds. During one incident, a door shut somewhere in the back. Another time, on one of the hottest summer days in New Mexico, she was enveloped in ice-cold air from head to toe. Goosebumps erupted all over her arms and she shivered, partly from the cold but also from fear.

Despite freaking out, she was able to chalk events like those up to the age of the building and her mind playing tricks on her. The last time she was here, showing the place to a very motivated buyer, something whispered in their ears. She had no idea what the thing had said but it was enough to creep her out when the client looked at her, indicating he'd heard the voice as well. They both left in a hurry.

No offer was made.

Addison scanned the area. It was quiet. She began to calm down.

"They'll be here in a few minutes. We won't be long."

Addison rested her hands on the counter. She felt the desert dirt cling to her palms. Ick. She looked down to see how dirty her hands had become but something else drew her attention. The dust, just above her hands, moved. It looked like an invisible finger was dragging through it.

GET OUT, it spelled and then a full handprint impression appeared next to the warning.

Addison ran.

2

ADDISON SCROLLED through the endless drivel on Craigslist. She had no idea where to begin. You can't go to the phonebook anymore to look up your local ghostbusters despite what the movies tell you.

She decided to simply search the term, 'ghost'. There was a cadre of results across the Craigslist spectrum for the term. Addison could have bought local, fresh ghost peppers. She could have purchased boxes of old books about ghosts. And, to add insult to injury, a complete set of Ghostbusters (the cartoon) action figures were available. Oh, the irony.

Then an ad, buried several pages in, caught her eye. It read: "Television Production seeking homeowners who experience paranormal activity on their property. Paranormal investigation free of charge for eligible candidates."

Addison re-read the ad copy. This sounded like what she was looking for, she thought. There wasn't anything about getting rid of the ghosts, but a free investigation to let her know if she was crazy or not? She knew she wasn't crazy. She knew what she experienced, but if this was going to be on television and she could show the world she wasn't losing her mind, that would be a step in the right direction. Hell, if she got the Hamburger House on television, it could help her sell as well.

She steeled herself and clicked the 'REPLY' button. The act of responding to the ad made the idea of a haunting at her real estate listing that much more real.

Her reply was short: "I'm answering your ad seeking properties with paranormal activity. I am a real estate agent representing a commercial property. I've experienced several occurrences while showing the restaurant. I am interested in your offer for a free investigation."

She clicked 'SEND' and felt stupid.

Paranormal investigation? How corny! Addison had been frightened of the boogeyman in her closet and the monster under the bed when she was a little girl. But, like everyone else, she grew up and understood there were practical reasons for houses making odd creaks and groans in the dead of night. Foundations settled. Wind blew through eaves. There was always a reasonable explanation. Ghosts weren't real. They just weren't.

Hamburger House had her thinking otherwise. Despite what she'd been through, there had to be a reasonable explanation. She wanted to look into the previous owners of the property. Maybe there was some sort of fraud taking place or they were trying to scare off the real estate agent so the property would be left in limbo again and they could swoop in and take ownership of the place for next to nothing.

That was the idea with The Amityville Horror house, right? Just some owners trying to get out of a bad real estate transaction.

Hamburger House was categorized as an abandoned property for at least two decades. It had been sitting so long with no interest, even the bank let it go. That's where Addison stepped in. Fresh off passing the licensing test to become a commercial real estate agent in the state of New Mexico, she sought out properties exactly like Hamburger House.

Old office buildings were prime pickups. They were hard to find and usually bought off short sales before they ever went into abandonment. Failed gas stations and service garages were pretty easy to find in this part of the country. Addison had found two within her first week in the business. They weren't useful for their intended purposes but often the lots could be sold to venture capitalists who would speculate the land for oil drilling or even the possibility of large real estate ventures like vacation resorts or mega shopping malls.

Addison picked up Hamburger House after the two quick gas station deals. Hamburger House was different right away. Its location, at the corner of two county roads, had some level of appeal. Sure, the nearby interstate carried traffic past the site at high speed but, if she could get some other businesses to pop up at the intersection, it could attract visitors once again.

All it needed was a gas station on an opposing corner to attract interstate travelers low on fuel. Maybe a souvenir type store in an adjacent lot. A truck stop would be fantastic, but getting the local board of trustees to agree to heavy truck traffic in this part of the sandbox was a hard sell. Plus, there were truck stops at the interstate exits east and west of Hamburger House.

Besides, all of that wouldn't matter if the ghosts of Hamburger House kept scaring off all potential buyers.

This place is not haunted.

Addison paced the room and refreshed her in-box with a compulsion reserved for people who suffer from ADD.

This place is not haunted.

She combed her fingers through her hair, manic. Why was there no reply? Was it a scam? Maybe she wasn't convincing enough. Maybe she should have added more detail. Maybe she already said too much. Ghosts can't be real. She was being a lunatic.

Addison cried out loud, "The place is not haunted."

Her computer bleeped. There was a reply in her inbox.

3

———

THE REPLY CAME:

> *Interested in your case. Please call (555) 555-5555.*
> *-Meshy, Not Normal Investigations/Not Normal Productions*

ODD, ADDISON THOUGHT. THE PHONE NUMBER SEEMED FAKE. THAT'S the type of phone numbers they give out on TV shows so that nobody calls an actual phone number. Her heart sank. This felt like a scam.

Yet, she swiped the unlock pattern into her cell phone and pressed the '5' ten times on the dial pad.

She waited to hear the tell-tale tones followed by a mechanical female voice saying that the line is not in service, check the number and dial again. Instead, she heard a man say, "Yello?" on the other end.

Addison was startled, "Ah, yes. Yellow. I mean, hello. My name is Addison Wilson. I'm the real estate agent that contacted you on

Craigslist. I'm calling you about the commercial property I discussed in my message."

"Ahh yes. Miss Wilson. You're the one with the haunted office or something."

"You can just call me Addy, mister..."

"Name's Tucker but you can call me Meshy."

Meshy? "Ok, ahh Meshy, the property is actually a restaurant, not an office. It's a commercial property, not residential. I didn't know if that matters or not?"

"Nope." Meshy said, popping the 'p' at the end of the word. "In fact, that's the appeal for us. We're shooting for a television show. It'll be good to have something different than a rickety, old house to feature in an episode. A restaurant sounds just weird enough."

"Oh, good. Great then!"

"What type of activity have patrons been experiencing?"

"Oh, well, the restaurant isn't open. In fact, it's been abandoned for a long, long time. Like I said, I'm the real estate agent for the property so it's just me that's been... experiencing things."

"Ahh okay. A little less exciting but go ahead, tell me about it."

Addison went over all the things she'd experienced. Her voice jittered as she recounted the event she experienced the day before. That was the first time she was alone in Hamburger House. She told Meshy she had no intentions of going back in until something could be done about the weird things that kept happening.

"Tell me something Addy, do you believe there's ghosts? Because, while your experiences do sound enticing, it also sounds like you don't want to believe what you've gone through."

The place is not haunted.

"I'm not a believer, not in ghosts Mr. Meshy."

"Just Meshy, ma'am."

"Sorry. I don't normally believe in ghosts but things keep happening to me. I want to believe it's not just me. The place is creepy and working on my imagination. I saw an invisible hand drawing in the dust. I *saw* it with my own eyes. How do I explain that?"

"Ya got ghosts is what ya got Addy."

Addison let out a soft whimper.

"Tell ya what. You've got a unique place there. I'd have preferred the place was operational. Getting patrons to recount their stories would have made great television. But you sound freaked out enough that I think we've got some bonafide paranormal activity there. Let's go ahead and make arrangements for me and my team to come out and conduct an investigation at your restaurant. What's the name of it?

"It's the old Hamburger House, right off Route 40, on 66 in Bard."

"Bard! Hooey, you are out in the middle of nowhere. Hamburger House? Haunted Hamburger House, great name for an episode."

Addison and Meshy agreed to meet at Hamburger House in a few days. Addison felt better, she wouldn't have to return to the place again. Not until Meshy and his team did away with the ghosts inside.

4

ADDY SHOWED up ten minutes late. She wanted to be sure Meshy and his crew got to Hamburger House first. There was no way she was going to stand on that lot alone before anyone else arrived.

This place is not haunted. She said it to herself as she pulled into the dusty parking area in front of the old building. She parked next to an older model minivan. The van had one remaining faux wooden panel on its rear quarter. On the driver's side door, she saw letters advertising it as NOT N RMAL INV S IGATIO S, LLC.

Addison didn't know if the missing letters were ironic, either way, her first impression was less than favorable.

The driver of the van opened his door. He wore a black baseball cap, the kind with mesh in the back, Von Dutch style, "Addy?"

Addison nodded, "You must be Meshy?"

"Yep."

The side door of the minivan slid open. A disheveled looking guy stepped out. He was holding a camera and had some other gadgets strapped around his neck like gaudy jewelry.

"That's my tech, Bucky Trott. You can just call him Bucky. Say hi, Bucky."

Bucky nodded at Addison, "Hi Bucky." he said.

Addison found him obnoxious and a little cute at the same time. She nodded back but didn't offer to shake his hand since they looked occupied with all manner of equipment.

From the passenger side of the van a woman emerged. She was pretty. Real pretty. Addy disliked her right away. The woman wore big, bug-eyed sunglasses that hid her true intention and her skin gleamed like toasted gold in the rising New Mexican sunlight.

"That's Paloma. Paloma, this is Addison Wilson. She prefers you call her Addy."

Addy grumbled. Paloma couldn't call her Addy, but it was too late.

Another gentleman emerged from the back of the van behind Bucky. He looked more like he was ready for safari than ghost busting. He wore tan khakis and matching work boots whose laces were tied in mirror images of one another. He had a salt and pepper beard that looked trimmed to precision.

"That's Basil." Meshy said, throwing a dismissive thumb in Basil's direction as he reached back inside the van to grab something.

"Hello, Basil." Addy thought Basil gave off the least creepy vibe of the quartet.

"Good morning Ms. Wilson. Thank you for having us," Basil offered.

Meshy pulled a hard-shell case from inside the van and moved to the rear and opened the hatch. "You can go on ahead and open up shop Addy. We're going to get some initial coverage of the outside before we venture inside and decide how we wanna do this thing."

"I, uhm, I'd prefer to stay out here if it's okay with everyone?" Addison said.

Bucky and Basil looked at Meshy. Paloma adjusted her sunglasses as she checked herself in the reflection of the van's windows.

"Ahh, c'mon Addy. You can't sit this out. You're our only witness. We've got nothing else to work with unless you can get us in there and show us around. Point out spots where stuff has happened to you. Without it there is no show and if there is no show, there is no investigation."

Meshy waited for Addison to move. She didn't

"Should we just pack up and leave then?"

Addy's shoulders slumped. "No. No, please stay. Can we just wait until we're all ready to go in though?"

Meshy opened his mouth to answer but Basil cut him off, "That'll be fine Ms. Wilson."

5

BUCKY WAITED until Addy was out of ear shot. She'd walked over to her car and started talking to someone on her phone. "She's kinda hot, eh Meshy?"

Meshy was rolling a piano out the back of the minivan. "Too old for you, too young for me."

"Aww c'mon. She can't be more than a few years older than me."

"Yeah, and that's a few too many. We've got work to do. Keep your mind on your job, not the eye candy. You know the show hinges on this job or we're sunk."

Bucky piped down having been verbally whacked on his nose.

"Give me a hand with this piano." Meshy called to Paloma, still primping herself in the van's window.

"Not in my contract," Paloma said without pausing her self-preening ritual.

"Basil. C'mon. You can do something other than break my balls."

Basil got behind the piano and helped push the upright across the pebbly parking lot to the front door. He didn't say anything, he didn't have to. Meshy would ask the question but if Basil offered his opinion before, it would break unspoken protocol.

"You have to be feeling something?" Meshy asked the question they both knew was coming.

"Just an old burger joint, so far."

"You're such a wet rag, you know that, Basil?" Meshy walked back to the van.

Basil shrugged. He didn't understand why Meshy got so irritated with him. He was hired to be the skeptic. He was the litmus test for their findings. Sure, it wasn't Meshy's idea to hire a skeptic but the network told him he'd need one for the show to work.

Meshy huddled up the Not Normal team at the back of the mini-van. "Okay, we only got Addy over there for eyewitness accounts. Let's set her up next to the front door since she's uneasy about this place. We'll get her to tell some stories before we go in. Tweak up her fear so maybe she'll give us some gold once we get inside."

Bucky nodded. Paloma remained steel-faced. Basil had nothing to protest, yet.

"Bucky, keep rolling when we're done with the interview. We'll get her to go inside first, Stay tight behind her, an over-the-shoulder shot. I'll follow in close behind you. Paloma, Basil, you two come in behind the rest of us. If any of you get any reactions when we walk in, save them for yourself. If I'm guessing correctly, Addy over there is gonna give us all the material we need right away."

"We want the meters running when we go in?" Bucky asked.

"No. Just reactions at first. We'll run the equipment after Addy shows us around a bit."

Meshy called Addy over. Addison lingered on her phone call. Meshy was feeling something about this Hamburger House. He didn't know if it was based on the real estate agent's apprehension or if there was something tickling his senses already.

Addy finally got off her phone and joined the crew. Meshy went over the plan, holding back the part about hoping she would freak the fuck out for the cameras.

Addy was worried, no doubt about it. She kept asking if they would be staying close. She made it clear she would not be walking into Hamburger House alone. She asked again if they could go in and investigate the place without her.

The answer, of course, was no.

They walked up to the front of Hamburger House. There was a faded logo painted on the glass pane of the door. They framed Addison in the shot so the logo could be seen as well.

Addy looked like she was ready to bolt. Meshy got Bucky recording and asked Addy some preliminary questions about the old restaurant. Not the ghosts, just the building and what she knew about it.

Addison told the story of how she came to be the agent of the building when Paloma cut in, "We're being watched," she said.

6

"OKAY, I'M DONE," Addison said, scooting away from the front door.

Meshy threw his hands up, "Jesus, Paloma! Did you have to spook her? You can tell she's on edge."

"What? We *are* being watched." Paloma pointed across the road.

Meshy chased after Addy, not paying attention to what Paloma was pointing out. Basil and Bucky spotted them though. There were two figures, in the distance, across the interstate. It looked like a black van had pulled to the side of the road.

"They're watching us with binoculars," Paloma said, "I caught the flash of the lens reflection."

Bucky squinted, "Who are they?"

"Doesn't matter," Basil said, "You already messed up the shot."

"Me?" Bucky protested.

"No," Basil said, "Paloma. You know better than to start with the medium stuff in the middle of a set-up."

"What medium stuff, darling? There are people up there watching us. You can see them as well as I do. No ghosts. That's your gig, right? Trying to prove we're a bunch of tricksters and there aren't spirits among us? Well," she pointed back to the two figures watching them, "there's your proof. No ghosts."

Basil shook his head.

Meshy was back with Addy. "Paloma. Please do not cut into a segment like that anymore. I've warned you before."

Paloma whipped her hair over her shoulder, not saying if she agreed or disagreed to those terms.

Meshy checked out the two people out across the sand. "Probably just a couple of locals. There's never any action in this no-horse town. Our little venture is enough to bring 'em out. Don't you worry none Addy. We get this kinda attention all the time."

Meshy got Addy framed in the shot as before. He suggested they roll a new take. They could piece stuff together in post-production.

Addison went on talking about Hamburger House. She had some general knowledge about the history of the place. She shared common knowledge about business along the old Route 66. The big interstate, out in the distance, bypassed the road and everything on it. Most businesses and the towns around them died slow deaths. Hamburger House was just another victim.

"Know anything about the original owners?" Meshy asked, trying to pry more out of Addy.

"No. I never really looked into it. Might be worth it, having some history to sell to my clients."

"Or to have some history to sell to our viewers," Meshy added, looking at Basil, "Why don't you see if you can dig into some of the old records on this place."

Basil nodded, pulling out his phone. Being the team skeptic also left him with less glamorous jobs, like research. At least, most historic records would be available digitally nowadays and he wouldn't have to take a ride to the nearest local library to go through microfiche rolls of old newspapers to dig up the dirt.

Meshy told Bucky they had enough from Addy to get started. Normally, they'd move their equipment into the house they were investigating and get a feel for the layout and the shots they could get before rolling. But Meshy suspected that Addy was going to spaz out when they walked in the burger joint. He didn't want to lose that shot.

"Bucky, get the handheld ready. Addy, we're going to go inside now. I'm going to have you walk in first..."

"Nope! Uh-uh." Addison said before the words were out of Meshy's mouth.

"Addy. You know you've got to do this for us. We're right here with you but you have to lead the shot. We'll be inches behind you. Just walk in there and point out the places you've experienced activity and that's it. We can take it from there."

"I can't. I can't go in there. This place is not haunted. It's not haunted."

Meshy was confused. "What do you mean, it's not haunted? That's why you called us out here. That's why you're so freaked out right now. There's something going on in there."

"I know," Addy cried, "But, if I say it. There's got to be an explanation."

"You're right. There's an explanation. That's why we're here, to investigate and get you an explanation. Right?"

Addy took a deep breath and slid the key into the lock. Meshy pushed Bucky behind Addy, rolling his finger to make sure he had the camera recording. Bucky nodded, framing his shot in the view finder with one eye and taking a peek at Addison's curves in her gray pencil skirt with the other.

The lock clicked open and the camera picked up Addy saying, "This place is not haunted." as she pushed the door open.

7

ADDISON LED the camera crew inside Hamburger House. She did her best to keep talking. The more she talked the less she focused on her fears.

She led them into the dining area first. She stopped and turned to face the camera for the first time, explaining how she once stood in this area with a client when she'd heard a voice saying something. She didn't think she'd really heard a voice until she looked at her client whose face said he'd heard the same thing. Chills ran up her spine recounting the event. She didn't mention that on camera.

Before the urge to bolt consumed her, she led the crew to a door next to the front counter and took them into the kitchen. She recalled how the kitchen looked when she first viewed the property for herself. There were mummified French fries in the warming bin. Tubs of preserved condiments were still stowed under hamburger prep tables. Any perishables left behind, had expired so long ago that it no longer left a stench. There were no lingering hamburger patties. She assumed the desert rats had consumed them long ago.

In the kitchen, she experienced equipment turning on by itself. The fryolator in particular, powered up on two different occasions.

There was no oil to heat but the built-in timers bleeped and red indicator lights lit up the control panel. It wasn't uncommon for the power company to keep electricity to vacant lots on to keep security and emergency equipment running in case of fire or break-ins. She'd chalked this activity up to shorted wiring or something.

To end her little tour of the Hamburger House, she led the group up front from the kitchen to the service counter. She wouldn't go near the cash register where she experienced the last incident. She pointed down the end of the counter and would only say that something had happened that really freaked her out.

Her heebie jeebies had reached full max. She wanted out. She broke her real estate agent role and said she was done. That's all she would show them, she was leaving.

"That's good Addy. That's all we needed," Meshy said. "We'll start setting up for the investigation. Let's all go outside and get some air."

The dry, dusty air inside made his throat scratchy. Not only that but, the fifteen minutes they'd just spent getting a tour was enough to convince Meshy that this hamburger joint was hopping. He'd felt tingles and cold spots, tell-tale signs of paranormal activity. And there was that unnerving feeling of being watched. Ghosts for sure.

They all followed Addy outside.

Bucky started moving cases and crates of their stuff inside the lobby.

Paloma kept one eye on the two figures still watching from across the sands and the other eye on her hair in the reflection of the window of Hamburger House. Basil sat on his case, scrolling through his phone. He'd found some property records, available on digital files on the county web site.

"Ms. Wilson? You did say that equipment had turned itself on a few times?"

"Yeah," Addison said. "Why?"

"Well, says here, power has been cut to this lot for about fifteen years now."

"Chief!" Bucky called from inside, "We've got a live one!"

Meshy ran back inside. Basil and Paloma followed behind as if rushing to a fire. Addison took a step away from the building.

Bucky pointed to the fryolator. He didn't have to; they could hear the alarms beeping from the lobby.

8

"BUCKY! CAMERA. NOW!" Meshy switched into investigator mode. Or maybe full-on director mode. Either way, he was missing an opportunity to capture his ghost.

Bucky ran for the camera, which he'd left outside while dragging in the rest of the equipment. Meshy moved toward the fryolator with a care reserved for approaching dangerous, wild animals.

Paloma and Basil observed from the lobby.

Meshy wasn't frightened. He'd been through this hundreds of times before. Things powered themselves up all the time. Or, to be more accurate, spirits powered things up all the time. Spirits were raw energy, kinetic and playful. Not always playful, sometimes inquisitive and sometimes malevolent. That was the key to paranormal investigations, finding out which type of energy was being released.

A beeping fryolator did not reveal the intent of the presence inhabiting Hamburger House. He approached, taking measured steps on the balls of his feet because you can spook a spook. It was his experience that a presence may be as unaware of the existence of the living as the living was unaware of the existence of the presence.

If you rushed to their activity, they could become startled and you'd lose the opportunity to capture the activity.

Meshy was behind the counter, creeping closer to the fryolator. Where was Bucky with the camera? Damn that kid, he should've known to have that camera ready!

"Got it!" Bucky said, running up to Meshy, camera on his shoulder, already recording.

The fryolator stopped beeping and went dark.

"Damnit Bucky! Dammit! You know not to run around like a cat that's seen a pickle!"

"What's that supposed to mean?" Bucky asked.

"A cat that's seen a pickle! Jesus, Bucky, don't you watch the internet? There's literally hours and hours of videos of cats coming upon pickles and they freak the fuck out like you just did!"

Bucky put the camera down and reached for the phone in his pocket.

Meshy smacked him across the arm, "I don't mean go looking for the videos now! Pick the fucking camera up and don't you dare put it down for the rest of the day. You got it? If you put that camera down again, you're off this crew!"

Bucky tucked his head down deep into his shoulders. He fucked up and he knew it. Meshy could be excitable at times, telling him to do three different things at once. Bucky was exceptional at doing one thing at a time. When the orders started piling up, he'd get downright confused. He picked the camera back up, wishing it had wi-fi so he could check out the cat pickle videos.

"Roll." Meshy instructed Bucky.

"Paloma," Meshy called out to the lobby, "You got anything?"

Paloma reached up and removed her sunglasses. She saw the villainess in a Bond movie make that gesture and she turned it into her signature move on the show. "I'm not picking up anything concrete. There's lots of static in the air. The spirits are still apprehensive, but they are here."

Paloma was the medium. She could commune with the spirits. All telepathic. It was another way the spirits cast out their energies.

Paloma was the antenna, picking up those energies like radio waves, feeding them back to Meshy and the audience at home. Meshy wanted to know if she picked up anything while the fryolator was acting up. If she hadn't, well, it could mean a lot of things or nothing at all. She'd never tell you she felt nothing, that made boring television and she knew it.

"Basil?" Meshy asked, filling the requirement for a skeptic's point of view.

"We'll have to check for battery power. This property hasn't had electricity for many years. There could be a backup generator running off propane. The fryolator is probably shorted out."

"Thanks, Donny Downer." Meshy said on camera, sure to get his dig in and make it clear to the folks watching at home that Basil was the enemy in this, and, in every episode.

Meshy framed himself in the lens, "We experienced some kitchen equipment turning itself on and off while setting up for our investigation. Basil has found that the utilities to Hamburger House have been turned off for many years. Paloma is not hearing anything yet. But we have activity early into our investigation, so there is no doubt that there are presences in this restaurant and they are ready to talk."

Meshy gave the signal to cut. Bucky stopped rolling. He held the camera at his side.

A golden opportunity had been missed but, like Meshy had said, the ghosts were eager to talk.

9

"OKAY, let's start out with the basics, meters and strobes. Set 'em up around the fryolator," Meshy ordered. "Basil, keep digging on history. See if we can find someone who might've worked here back in the sixties or seventies. Paloma, keep reaching out, if you get anything, I want to know immediately. And Bucky, keep that fucking camera on you at all times. I don't wanna miss another event. Got it?"

The rest of the crew nodded and set off on their tasks.

Meshy strolled around the restaurant. He had to admit, it brought some pangs of nostalgia back. The tables and booths in the lobby were upholstered with red and white vinyl but looking at them he could see them, bright and new, like he was a kid again and this was every burger joint his parents had ever treated him to. Wooden paneling, the hallmark of cookie cutter class decor of the sixties and seventies, still looked to be in good shape, if not completely out of its time today.

There were pictures hung around the lobby. Pure Americana if he'd ever seen it. One picture was a Rockwell-inspired piece depicting a man in pristine kitchen white linen, complete with a paper soda jerk hat, handing a bag out his service window to an eager little boy wearing a collared shirt, shorts and brown shoes and his hair tousled, so we all know the kid was all about playing and having fun. Another picture showed a cow, a tomato, a head of lettuce and a Coke in four quadrants. The picture made Meshy smile. This was his kind of art gallery.

He wandered along, lost for a moment in this museum of memorabilia. The next picture he came upon grabbed his attention. It was different from the rest. A clown, in portrait. He wore a blue, felt hat with a white pom-pom on top and matching blue jumper. His face make-up was black features on white and his smile was painted-on big, there was no mistaking this was a happy clown. And yet, Meshy couldn't help but see sadness in the clown's face. It was disturbing.

"Bucky, come here." Meshy said, not taking his eyes off the portrait.

Bucky was setting up the EMF meter next to the fryolator. Basil was helping him, "You better get over there, I'll finish up." Basil said, continuing to set up the equipment he didn't believe worked the way the rest of the crew believed it did.

Bucky got up to go see what Meshy wanted.

"Bucky," Basil called, "Camera."

"Right!" Bucky said, "Thanks!"

Bucky grabbed the camera and met Meshy at the portrait.

"Oh good," Meshy said, "you got the camera this time. Did you bring the tripod?"

Bucky melted, "No."

"Okay, just give me the camera and go get the tripod. I wanna roll on this picture for a little bit while we finish setting up at the fryolator. There's something about this picture..."

Bucky handed the camera over and ran to grab the tripod.

Meshy held the viewfinder at eye level and observed the picture through the lens. The clown still wore a big, black smile but now he looked startled somehow. Like, maybe his eyebrows raised a bit and somehow his lips were pursed more in an 'o' shape. And yet, the picture was static. There was something up.

Bucky was back with the tripod.

"I think we may have found who's been messing with the fryola-tor," Meshy said, mounting the camera on top of the legs. "Just let the camera roll for a while. I'll help you guys finish setting up the equipment. You brought the eggs, right?"

"Yeah Meshy. I brought 'em." Bucky said and they moved away from the picture.

When they ran the playback later, they'd find that the picture growled at them as they walked away.

"We're here. Do you wanna talk to us?" Meshy asked the fryolator.

The fryolator didn't speak.

"Are you trying to talk to us? This is your chance. We are here to listen to you. We won't run away."

Bucky scanned the spirit detection array they'd set up around the fryolator. There was an EMF meter that picked up fluctuations in the electro-magnetic field. They'd also set up two small plastic eggs, one marked YES and the other No. The eggs had little sensors inside them that would trigger a tiny strobing LED light inside if they were disturbed in any way. In theory, the energies could manipulate the eggs to communicate simple yes/no answers to the Not Normal Investigations team. Last, they'd set up a thermal scanner that constantly monitored the temperature around the fryolator and would sound an alarm if the ambient temperature spiked up or down. Temperature fluctuations and paranormal activity always went hand in hand.

All their equipment remained quiet.

Meshy continued reaching out to the potential energies in the restaurant, "Did you work at Hamburger House? Were you the fry guy?"

The thermal scanner went off. Paloma leaned into the shot, reading the spike. "Cold spot, thirty Fahrenheit. I'm not feeling anything. Temperature is ambient again."

Meshy got his hit, he continued his line of questioning, "Did you enjoy your job? Did you have fun working at Hamburger House?"

They waited for the fryolator to answer. For a moment, it was quiet again.

"The egg. No!" Paloma called out, pointing to the strobing light.

Meshy honed in, "You didn't like the job? Did you like your boss?"

They waited. Nothing.

"Was it the customers? Did someone mistreat you?"

Paloma pointed to the NO egg. It was flashing again. They were getting some decent activity. It was best to stay quiet now that the activity was ramping up. If too many people started talking, the energy could lose focus or be spooked off.

"Did someone do something to you here at the restaurant? Did you die here?"

The EMF meter and the thermal scanner were both set off at the same time.

Meshy's eyes lit up. Major activity. He was definitely in contact with the presence. And he'd hit on some possible explanations for the activity going on in Hamburger House.

"Can you turn on the fryolator for us? Maybe you want to cook something for us?"

Meshy was trying to elevate the activity. The spirits could trigger their simple equipment without much effort, even the Yes/No eggs didn't require much manipulation from the energy. But to get the presence to turn on the kitchen equipment, that would require a bigger expenditure of energy, and would be a gem for this segment of the investigation.

"You turned it on before. Were you trying to get our attention when we walked outside? You seem like you want to talk to us."

The NO egg twinkled once more.

"No? You don't want to talk to us? But you are, you're talking to us right now."

The presence went silent. Meshy continued to ask it to turn on the fryolator or talk to them. The instruments all went quiet. The moment had passed.

"It's gone quiet. Paloma, were you getting anything at all during that?"

"Still nothing. The spirit was curious about our equipment, that's for sure. I'll continue to keep reaching out."

Meshy deferred to Basil, the party pooper, for his contractually obligated naysaying.

"I don't know that we had authentic spirit communication. There were two, very brief thermal events. It could have been a breeze or miscalibration." Basil offered.

"You're telling me there could be a thirty-degree breeze inside an abandoned restaurant in the middle of the New Mexico desert?"

Basil shrugged, "Same for the EMP meter. Electromagnetic fluctuations occur all the time. I can't confirm a paranormal event on one abnormal reading."

"We had a lot of interaction with the Yes/No eggs."

"Actually, you only had activity with the NO egg. Again, they are set to activate on the slightest motion or manipulation. There are always errant air currents or even minor seismic activity."

"Or," Meshy said, a little perturbed, "maybe the answer was No to all my questions."

Basil rolled his eyes, "Maybe."

"Well, that's your opinion. This investigation is indicating significant paranormal activity, regardless. Basil, I'm going to need you to see if you can find anything about former employees dying while at work at Hamburger House. As we've just learned, there may be some foul play afoot."

Bucky stopped recording. Their first investigative session was a success. They captured a bit of activity. They could break for a bit before moving onto the next segment.

ADDY SAT IN HER CAR, door open, feet out the side, planted in the dusty gravel. The New Mexican sun seared the desert sands. She wished she had a cigarette. She hadn't smoked in almost a decade. There were none available to her right now or she'd be back to a pack-a-day habit in the flick of a Bic.

She wished she could leave the Not Normal Investigations crew to do whatever it was they were doing inside Hamburger House. The heat was beginning to get to her. She was accustomed to the desert sun but blazing hot was blazing hot by anyone's standards. Maybe she could shoot down 66 into San Jon and eat inside an operational burger joint, soak up some air-conditioned relief over a frozen milkshake.

Addison was a professional, damn it. It would be irresponsible to leave the property unattended. If there was any sort of accident, she would be liable. If the insurance company found out she left a crew of ghost hunters to poke around the abandoned building while she was off in the next town, enjoying a cold beverage, well, that would be the end of her coverage, her license and her livelihood.

If she wasn't so frightened of what was happening inside

Hamburger House, she could duck out of the sun and observe the investigation they were conducting. Nobody had come running out, screaming for their lives. She didn't hear any equipment beeping or other types of unholy sounds.

Maybe her ghosts were shitheads. Maybe they only disliked her. Perhaps they were all in there having a spot of tea with the spirits and laughing at how scared the poor, innocent real estate agent had become over their little tricks.

Addy stood up. Enough, she was going to go in and see what was happening. She took two steps and froze. The fear crippled her.

This place is not haunted. This place is not haunted. This place is not haunted.

Her feet moved again. She repeated the mantra to herself. She got herself to the sidewalk, only a few steps from the front door. She was screaming the mantra, louder and louder, drowning out every other voice in her head imploring her to run.

The front door opened. Basil and Bucky walked out.

Bucky smiled at Addy, "Hey, we just finished up the first segment. It went great!"

"Oh! Good, good. Did you, uh, find anything?"

Bucky smiled bigger. Addy was taken aback. He was fucking cute as hell when he smiled that big.

"Yeah, we got some stuff. Wanna see?" Bucky asked, bringing the camera's tiny monitor up to Addy's point of view.

Addison backed up and turned her eyes away. She didn't want to see.

"Oh, sorry Addy. I'm used to them. The ghosts, that is. There's really nothing to be scared of, they're usually just playing around, ya know?"

"Not the... whatever it is in there. It acts mean. I never felt like whatever's going on in there was just trying to have some fun."

Basil stepped in, "Addison, I'm on your team here. You're apprehensive about there even being ghosts or spirits or energy inside that restaurant. I'm with you on that. Whatever Bucky says we caught on camera just now is easily explained. You've just gotta believe what you've gotta believe, given the facts." He clapped Addy on the back and walked over to the van. He had some more research to conduct.

"He's supposed to say that stuff. But I've seen enough facts to know that sometimes, the only explanation is ghosts."

Addy knew Bucky was trying to make it better, but he didn't. Even if he did have an adorable smile.

Meshy came out with Paloma. They were talking about a picture and recordings. Paloma drew her attention away from what Meshy was talking about, looking off at the two men by the van. They were still there, looking back.

"Have they been there the whole time?" Paloma asked Addy.

Addison hadn't been paying that much attention to the two men while she waited in the parking lot. "Yeah, I guess so. I never saw them leave."

"If there's one thing I'm feeling, Meshy, it's that we're being watched."

"I told you Paloma, they're just curious locals. Don't let them distract you. This place is hot, I need you to focus on picking up what's going on here, not off in the desert."

"Do you know anything about anyone who may have worked here at one time?" Meshy asked Addy, turning his attention away from Paloma, who was laser-focused on the two men out in the desert.

"Ahh, no? This place has been closed down longer than I've been alive."

"I thought, maybe, you've heard stories. Nothing?"

"Nothing other than what little I've already said. I know I can sell it to you for a steal, if you're interested. Maybe you could turn it into a ghost museum or something. Don't people sell haunted attractions all the time?"

Addy couldn't believe herself. She was in sales mode. She hadn't even put thought into the pitch at all, it just came natural to her. She had a haunted place to sell and Meshy struck her as someone who might be in the market for a haunted place to showcase. Win, win, all around.

Meshy just laughed, "I'm not in the tourist business Addy, though that's a fine idea. In fact, that may be the angle you need to sell this place. You seem to have a grumpy presence in there."

Addy slumped, "But you said you were going to get rid of the ghosts!"

"Whoa, whoa! I never said that. I don't claim to get rid of ghosts. I'm an investigator. You're getting a complimentary investigation in exchange for allowing us full access to the property to record our findings. That's the deal."

Addison became furious, "Why would I want you to come out here to investigate something I already know?" *This place is not haunted.* "There's fucked up shit going on in there. I know that already." *This place is not haunted!* "I don't need you to tell me what I already know. I need *you* to get in there and get them out so I can rid myself of this burden."

Oh God, this place IS haunted!

Addy broke down and started crying.

Bucky put a hand on her shoulder and rubbed. He didn't know what to say. They weren't ghostbusters. He felt awful about that. He felt awful for Addy.

"Meshy? Can't we try to do something? Sometimes, you know, you talk to them and try to make them move on, right?"

Meshy knew what Bucky was talking about. Sometimes a spirit was just stuck. They wanted to move on but something kept them where they were. That type of situation usually led to your poltergeist type hauntings.

"Listen, Addy, I'm sorry if I led you to believe we could do something more for you," Meshy said, trying to sound as comforting as he could muster, "but, that's just not our business. Like Bucky said, I can try to talk to them. See if, maybe, they would leave on their own volition. It's an unusual request, but this is already an unusual investigation."

"Fuck yeah! We're ghostbusters now!" Bucky said.

Addy looked at Bucky through her tears. He was smiling again, looking good. That made her feel a little bit better. "Okay," she said and kissed Bucky on the cheek, "Thank you."

Bucky rubbed the spot Addy touched her lips to, "Thank you," he said, awestruck.

12

PALOMA STARED down the two men across the desert. They were being watched. The trouble was she didn't believe they were just innocent locals scoping them out. They were different. Creepy different.

She felt it. The guys in the desert threw her off at first. She thought they made her psychic antenna buzz. But her senses tingled in a way they'd never done before. Her gut reaction was to blurt out their presence to everyone else.

She freaked Addy out. Paloma freaked herself out as well. She reigned in her emotions and played it off as if the two men watching them had triggered her outburst. But it wasn't. Paloma knew something else had set her off. She just happened to catch sight of the mysterious onlookers at the same moment she felt something else notice her and her receptors.

Meshy was right, of course. They attracted curious onlookers all the time. The show they were producing hadn't made it to TV, not yet. Still, when a group of strangers hung around the creepiest house in town, you tended to draw attention to yourselves. They welcomed it. It would create a buzz through the local grapevine and then get whispered across the social networks. They hoped the added attention would help land them a streaming deal with one of the big boys.

Those guys though, they weren't curious. They were observational. Nothing about them seemed like the nosey local type. They weren't raising her psychic hackles but she had a bad feeling about them nonetheless. She was surprised Meshy was blowing them off, he was usually good at picking up on negative vibes.

Basil was near to her. "What do you think of those two out there?"

Basil hesitated. He was focused on his phone. Doing research, no doubt. He was too smart for this job. They needed a skeptic, though. If they could get Basil to admit that, maybe, just maybe, one of their investigations was inexplicable, they had themselves a guaranteed season of a bonafide ghost hunting show.

"Huh," Basil asked, realizing Paloma was talking to him, "Sorry, I just found some stuff here. Something kind of interesting. What did you ask me?"

"Those guys that have been watching us. What does the skeptic think of them?"

Basil raised his hand over his eyes to shield the sun's glare and observed them for a moment. All he saw was the pair observing back. "I dunno. Watching us I suppose. We're in a two-horse town, it's easy to draw attention."

"There's something else. They've been out there watching us since we got here."

"Maybe Addy told them she was having people out to investigate. We don't know too much about her either, ya know?"

"Or maybe there's something they know about this place that Addy doesn't. You know how it is, everyone knows the haunted places in town. If strangers come poking around, they're going to get all giddy. Like we're going to find their ghosts."

"You don't believe in ghosts."

"No, but I understand that others believe in ghosts."

"Maybe. But the curious ones, they always come right up to us. Most aren't ashamed to ask what we're up to. That's real curiosity.

Those guys, they aren't curious. They're observing. That's what's bothering me."

Basil hesitated. "Hmm, you've got a point. You think we should get Meshy and take a ride over there?"

"Maybe. Not yet. What was it you said you found?"

Basil became excited, "Ahh, yes! I found the San Jon Gazette archives. It's a bitch to search but I hit on something kind of interesting. One article about a former employee of Hamburger House."

"Oh, good. Meshy will be happy to hear that. You think we can find the guy?"

"Doubtful," Basil said, showing Paloma the image capture of the article on his phone, "he's dead."

Paloma read the headline of the article: **Hamburger House Employee Found Deep Fried to Death**

MESHY GRABBED hold of Bucky as Addison stepped over to her car to take a phone call. This was the second time today he was going to have to dress this kid down. He didn't want to do that. He was a good kid. He didn't get freaked out by the spooky shit. That was an asset. He was also girl-crazy over Addy. That was a liability.

"What the hell, Bucky?"

"What did I do now, Meshy?"

"Ghostbusters? Are you for real?"

"Ahh, Meshy. C'mon, you see how upset Addy is, we've gotta help her."

Meshy got up into Bucky's face, "Let me do some basic math for you. *We* are trying to film a paranormal investigation show. Right?

Bucky thought about it for a moment, "Yeah."

"And in order for us to do that successfully, we need for there to be paranormal activity, okay?"

"Uh huh."

Meshy took it up a notch, "Then how the hell are we going to get paranormal activity for the show if we chase the god-danged ghosts away, Bucky?!"

"I know Meshy. But when we're done with the investigation. I just figured—"

"Don't figure. It's my job to figure. Your job is to roll camera and keep a visual record of our findings."

"And to lug the stuff out of the van. And to set it up."

"Yes, that stuff too. But your main job is to operate that camera. And keep your mind on your work and not on Addy. She'll be long gone after we're done here and onto our next job."

"Ahh, Meshy, it's not like that."

"It *is* like that, Bucky. That girl has your brain scrambled up like hot eggs. There'll be plenty of girls for you once we get this show on TV. But only if you keep your mind on your work so we can make the best show possible."

"Okay Meshy. But we're still going to try to help Addy, right? You said you would, you told her that."

Meshy sighed, "Yes, I said that. We'll try to help her out."

Bucky smiled, "Great! Do you want to set up for that segment with the painting now?"

Meshy decided that wasn't the best approach now. That painting gave him the heebie jeebies he'd not experienced in a long time. He decided it was time to break for lunch. Maybe even dinner too. He didn't want to do the painting segment until darkness crept over Hamburger House.

Everything was scarier in the dark.

14

ADDY LED the Not Normal Investigations team down Route 66 to San Jon. The town was adjacent to Bard and more of a town than Bard could ever hope to be. San Jon had a few truck stops. That's all you needed out here in the middle of nowhere to survive.

The restaurant Addy had chosen looked more like a children's daycare than a burger joint. There was a fenced in park to one side of the building. A drive-thru lane on the opposite side and the brick front was topped with a colorful red roof cap. They all knew the place. Everyone knew the place, they came to eat at a one-of-a-million burger chain, Not Donald's. You didn't have to see anything but the giant letters "ND" perched on the roof in bold yellow.

It wasn't much of a restaurant but San Jon wasn't much of a town. This was the closest place to grab a bite to eat. If you wanted to get fancy you had to drive another half hour or so west, into Tucumcari. Besides, everyone knew the name. They knew what was on the menu. It was the same from coast to coast. That's what made them a world-wide brand, global consistency. That and their stupid clown mascot that got kids hooked on the burgers right out of the womb.

"All right! Notty D's!" Bucky was as excited as an eight-year-old to have lunch at Not Donald's.

Addy wondered if he would order a kid's meal just to get the toy. She smiled, it was an adorable thought and she just might melt if he did wind up doing that. She glanced at the windows to see if they were advertising the toy of the month. Maybe it would be some masculine toy reboot from Bucky's not-too-distant childhood that was sure to appeal to him. There weren't any window clings, she'd have to wait with bated breath.

Everyone else piled out of the NNI van. Paloma was the first to voice her less-than-impressed opinion of the place. Addy didn't like that she was beautiful, it allowed her to have unfavorable opinions of fast-food joints. Basil and Meshy didn't seem to mind, and if they did, they put on a good show of it.

They walked in through the front door and were hit with cold air and loud children's music. They welcomed the cool air and pretended to tolerate the awful music. Not Donald's always played it up for the kids. It was a brilliant business model. Get the kids hooked, this way they demand their parents take them to eat there. Children were experts at pestering and parents had a low threshold for persistence. Sooner or later, they would crack and the family would be piled into the minivan for lunch or dinner at Not Donald's.

Let's not forget Neddy Not Donald, the clown that sold a billion hamburgers to happy children the world over. Neddy was the face of the chain. How could they resist? There was a life-sized fiberglass Neddy situated at the entrance to every Not Donald's. He smiled and waved to every guest, locked in a permanent, family friendly pose. An icon that rivaled Jesus Christ and The Mouse. If it weren't for Neddy Not Donald, the chain would never have found its footing and climbed to become a giant corporation with global reach. They would've floundered and died along Route 66 just like Hamburger House.

Bucky high-fived the clowns waving hand as he passed him on the way inside. Addy smiled. It's a move all the kids were doing these days, fueled by a Shok-Tok video that went viral. Now the whole world was high fiving the Neddy Not Donald statue and capturing the moment for their own Shok-Tok video feeds.

Addy pulled out her phone, "Hey do that again, I wanna put it up on my Shok-Tok."

Bucky laughed like a love-sick puppy. "Okay!" he went through the routine again so Addy could capture it to share with the rest of the internet. Like they hadn't seen it a million times before. "I didn't know you had a Shok-Tok. What's your name so I can follow you." Bucky asked as he whipped out his phone and opened the app.

"It's AddySells819." she told him.

"Got it! Awesome." Bucky said.

They had a connection now. Addy felt butterflies. She was falling for his naive boyish charm. She kind of hated herself and didn't care.

The others placed their order at the counter. Bucky ordered a NotMaxSupreme with large fries and a large pop. Addy was a bit disappointed he didn't go for the kid's meal. She ordered the NotBurger with side salad instead of fries and a water.

Their lunch was assembled with haste, the Not Donald's way. Before they knew it, they were all sitting around a double-long booth, scarfing down their lunch in relative silence.

Meshy was the first to start up the conversation, "So, the way I see it, we have two more segments to get." He looked across the booth to Addy, "Obviously, I want to focus on the most recent activity you experienced at the front counter."

Addy nodded. She was able to put on a smiling veneer because she wasn't near Hamburger House right now.

"But," Meshy continued, "there's a picture hanging in the dining area that's grabbed my attention. I had Bucky roll another camera on it while we recorded the fryolator segment. I'll check it when we get back, to see if it captured anything. Doesn't matter, there's something up with the picture. Have you had any experiences in the dining area Addy? Anything at all that maybe you forgot about?"

Addy gave it some thought. She never gave much thought to

where things had occurred, but when she plotted it out, it seemed most activity started at the front counter and behind, into the kitchen, office and walk-in freezer.

Most clients gave a cursory glance to the dining area. The expanse of it was visible when you walked-in the front door. There wasn't much to explore deeper. Everyone was interested in the meat and potatoes of the place. The spot where any real work would take place in the restaurant.

"Nothing comes to mind. No."

"What is it about that portrait that's gotten your attention Meshy? I wasn't getting so much as a single hair raised from it." Paloma asked.

"I dunno. Something in my gut. I didn't experience anything per se. I just thought maybe it had some life to it when I looked at it."

"Ha! Meshy the fine art connoisseur." Bucky laughed.

The last thing Meshy ever wanted to be compared to was some uppity, hoity-toity connoisseur of art. That wasn't him at all. Meshy was salt of the earth, through and through.

"Shut up," Meshy made it clear Bucky was being insubordinate, "I don't know the first thing about art. It's all splatter picture drawings to me."

Basil jumped in to take the heat off Bucky, "I found something on an employee at Hamburger House. It's an interesting story."

They all looked to the booth across from them where Basil sat, the odd man out.

He pulled up the article on his phone and read the headline he'd shown to Paloma earlier. Everyone forgot that Meshy almost teed off on Bucky.

Basil went on to recap the article. There was a guy by the name of Ko Nakha. He worked at Hamburger House from the first day it opened. According to this article he was a war hero, one of the old Navaho Code Talkers. After the war ended, talking in code wasn't work he could apply for in the real world, so he took a job at the restaurant.

Ko was a trusted employee. He was placed in charge of the

closing shift. He closed the place, every night, Monday through Saturday, without incident. That is, until the morning of May 30th, 1970. The owner showed up that morning to open the restaurant as he'd done every morning only to find the door was not locked and the lights were still on. Inside, he found a gruesome scene.

Ko was dead, plunged face first into the fryolator, black smoke billowing out of the bubbling oil. He'd been charred to a crisp, over-cooked for hours.

"The only thing local police found was a red rubber clown nose lying on the floor behind Ko's body." Basil finished.

"Holy shit." Bucky said.

"What?" Basil asked.

The picture that grabbed my attention in the lobby," Meshy explained, "It's a portrait of a clown."

"Speaking of clowns," Paloma interjected.

They all looked at Paloma. She nodded to the front counter. They all craned their heads in the direction she indicated and saw what must have been the world's oldest living clown, hunched over from years of bearing a clown's burden. He wore a red and yellow striped jumper, the signature colors of the Not Donald's brand. His head donned a big mop of curly, red hair. His painted-on smile face did little to hide the look of a tired old man. The clown make-up did little to smooth the wrinkles of an eternity of clowning.

"Holy shit," Meshy said, "it's..."

"Neddy Not Donald!" Bucky finished, as if Robert Downy, Jr. just showed up in full Iron Man regalia. He jumped out of the booth, "Addy, get your phone. I'm gonna go high five the real guy!"

Addy gushed. Bucky hit full boyish charm.

15

Two GUYS SAT in their van, watching nothing happen across the street at the Not Donald's.

"This job sucks, Number A."

"You got something better to do, Number B?"

Number B, sitting in the passenger seat, thought about the question. Number A didn't understand his hesitation. This was the cushiest job anyone could have ever had. All they had to do was watch and observe. Better yet, this particular assignment was to observe people who were observing ghosts. What could be easier?

"Nah, not right now. But one day, I wanna be my own boss," Number B said.

Number A snickered, "Oh yeah? Your own boss of what?"

"My own company. Doing what I wanna do."

"What is it you want to do?"

"Be my own boss."

Number A sighed. This job was too easy. They were losing focus. They weren't even watching their primary target. Instead, they were instructed to tail the ghost hunters. He didn't understand the directive. They were only out to lunch and had left their equipment at Hamburger House. The ghostbusters were sure to go back at some point. So why take their eyes off the prize just to watch a group of people chasing phantoms have lunch at a fast-food restaurant?

"Ever eat Indian food, Number B?" Number A asked, trying to make conversation.

"Yeah, I went to one of those Pow-Wows once. They had deep fried corn, deep fried rice, deep fried pumpkin and deep-fried alligator. The alligator was pretty good, actually. Tasted just like chicken."

"That's pretty racist, Number B."

"Racist? Eating alligator?"

"No! Thinking Native American food is Indian food. So racist. I can't believe you passed the agency background check."

"Oh, what's the difference? Indian, Native American. It's all food. Good, deep-fried food."

"Think about what you're saying Number B. Do you really think Native Americans were sitting around deep-frying corn and alligator while waiting for Christopher Columbus to arrive?"

"See, *that* sounds racist. You think Indians don't know how to deep fry food just because they live in tents and stuff? You're the racist Number A, not me."

"Wow," That's all the energy Number A had left in him.

"All this talk about food has got me hungry, Number A."

"So, eat your lunch. I'll keep an eye on them."

"I didn't bring lunch."

"Why didn't you bring lunch? You knew we were on reconnaissance today."

"Yeah, at a hamburger restaurant."

"You idiot. You know we can't just go into the place we're scoping out. We'd blow our cover."

"Not Donald's isn't the place we're scoping out."

"It is now."

"I could go for a Double NotMax with Double NotFries and a DoubleDoublePop Freeze."

Number A was frustrated with his partner, the new guy. He always got stuck with the new guy. The agency assured Number A that the kid scored aces on all his practicals. They said he had a military background. Top notch, the whole nine. All Number A got was another newbie.

He'd show Number B the ropes. They'd partner up for a year. Number B would get better, thanks to him. No help from the agency. That wouldn't stop them from promoting Number B, while Number A got left in the dust again.

It's the optics of the matter. Throw an inept idiot into a job and when he excels beyond expectations, that's the guy who gets promoted while the mentor gets left behind. A pat on the back, good job getting the rookie up to snuff. Rookie is going to go on to great things. You're good too but we need you here, in the shit. Who else do you think is going to train the next new guy?

Number A, that's who.

"Number B. This is a truck stop. Go to the gas station shop. I'm sure they've got some crap you can grab to eat. Maybe even a hot dog that's been rolling around on the grill for a few days. That ought to hold you over."

"Hold me over until what?"

"Until later."

"Then what are we going to eat?"

"*I'm* going to eat the food I packed. I'm prepared for everything. Just like they taught me in agent training. Didn't they go over this stuff with you?"

Number B shrugged. Maybe they had. He didn't know. He took the job after his last tour of duty. Anything to get out of the middle east. It was too hot out there. And the freaking creatures they had there? He saw some weird shit. Shit that looked out of this world. And that's why he took the job when it was offered.

An opportunity to work with things not of this world. Or something to that effect was how the job was presented to him. He figured he knew the territory. But, honest to goodness aliens? He wasn't expecting that. Plus, he figured it would get him out of the desert in Iraq.

And now here he was in the desert of New Mexico. And he was

hungry. And his partner was being a dick. He hated being the new guy, hungry in the desert.

He got out of the van, slamming the door shut. Number B was pretty sure he couldn't get in trouble for that action. He walked to the gas station store, shuffling his boots in the sandy gravel lot, kicking up a small dust storm.

He found a bag of nacho chips and some sort of soda. He was pretty sure it was orange but the words were all in Spanish. He returned to the van and ate like an ill-mannered five-year-old to spite Number A, who was eating a sandwich.

Number B wiped his orange fingers off on his khakis, leaving streaks, "I still don't know why we gotta keep an eye on this gang. They're ghost hunters. They ain't even looking for extraterrestrials."

Number A fixated on the cheese powder streaks on Number B's pants, "Because, they've got a psychic on that team. You didn't read the briefing, did you?"

Number B shrugged, "You read it. Good enough for me. Which one is it, the guy wearing the baseball hat?"

"Might be. Report doesn't specify."

"Maybe we need a psychic on *this* team to figure out who the psychic is on *that* team."

"That may be the best idea you've had all day."

Number B popped the cap off his soda pop, "See, I just needed some food to get the noggin working at full steam," he pulled a glug of pop. "Ahh," he said appreciating the cold drink, "too bad we can't just convince their psychic to be on our team."

Number A laughed. This guy wasn't so bad after all. "Wow, maybe you *did* read the briefing! That's exactly why we're out here."

16

THE NOT NORMAL Investigations team bounced scenarios about the feud between Ko Nahka and the clown. Instead of being creeped out, Addy found a lot of their theories quite entertaining.

Meshy was convinced that the clown was Ko Nakha's father, a lifelong member of a traveling circus. He wanted Ko to join him in the ways of clowning but Ko didn't want to follow in his father's footsteps. So, one night, while Ko was alone on the night shift, the clown snuck up on Ko and pushed him into the fryer.

That story was too contrived for Paloma. Though her psychic abilities had yet to tingle, she posited that the clown nose was a planted distraction. The in-house psychic for Not Normal Investigations insisted Ko was the victim of a Mexican drug cartel that was moving product through Hamburger House. The leader of the cartel was working with the owner of a fast-food joint and the staff was none the wiser. Until, one night, Ko found the stash as it was being fenced through the restaurant. Ko, a dedicated military man, threatened to go to the police. The cartel sent in their muscle and, in order to punish Ko and send a clear message to anyone else who would threaten their operation, an unthinkable death was bestowed upon the unfortunate war hero.

Bucky offered a love story for his theory. It was crude but he suggested that Ko was banging the boss's wife. The boss got pissed and stormed in to confront Ko, who had his wife bent over the fryer. They were going at it and the boss got so mad he ripped the clown nose off the restaurant mascot's face (because short order hamburger joints always employed clowns to draw in customers by Bucky's reasoning) and threw it at Ko. The nose, which Bucky felt must've been made with a higher density foam than they utilize nowadays, knocked Ko out cold and he fell face first in the fryer. Bucky also suggested they search the freezer, where they were certain to find the frozen ghost of the boss's wife who he hung like a side of beef until she froze to death.

Addy couldn't help but laugh at Bucky's hypothesis. It was oddly romantic if nothing else.

Basil didn't have a theory. He suggested further research. There were sure to be police reports. Perhaps the murder had even been solved and there were court documents that shared all the evidence presented in the case.

Addy thought that was boring but also, the closest to the real story. The storytelling had put them in good spirits. They egged Addy on for her version of Ko's story but she declined. She wasn't much of a storyteller, she liked hard numbers. She wasn't ashamed to admit she thought Basil's story was the most realistic one.

"Well of course it's the most realistic, it's the most boring," Meshy said, "But life isn't *always* boring. There's always pepper. Christ, if life wasn't spiced, why bother living it?"

"Sure, you're right. But, in this case, homicide? I've watched enough of the Crime ID channel to know that the simplest theory is usually the correct one. It's how you tell the truth that makes the story compelling. Fantastic explanations aren't always intriguing."

"Touché," Meshy raised his can of pop, "But, give me a good, old-fashioned ghost story over some lazy crime noir any day of the week."

"I've got a theory for ya," came the wobbly voice of an old man.

They all jumped. The clown had snuck upon them. He stood

hunched at the side of the table. How long had he been standing there?

Nobody asked him what his theory was, but he continued when he saw they had his attention, "Theory goes there was a clown, like me, out at the ol' Hamburger House. He stood out on the edge of '66 and waved at the motorists, all day and all night. Soon folks didn't need no wavin' in. They were compelled to turn into the burger stand, have themselves a bite to eat, and let the kids play with Crumbles Calhoun, the Hamburger House clown."

Meshy perked up, "The Hamburger House clown?"

The old man, dressed up as Neddy Not Donald grumbled. He was annoyed to have his story cut off. He continued without acknowledging Meshy's interruption, "Ol' Crumbles made that place what it was. And it wasn't just the kids and their parents that noticed. Someone else was watching Crumbles as well. Donny Donald himself."

Bucky's eyes widened, "Whoa, the founder of Not Donald's?"

Neddy Not Donald huffed, interrupted again, "Donny saw the dollars pouring in. He ran his own burger stand out in Albuquerque. Runnin' a burger joint was pretty standard stuff. So, what was Hamburger House doing that every other burger joint wasn't?" Neddy Not Donald craned his neck up and looked into their eyes, "The clown. That's what."

"So, Donny Donald became inspired by the Haunted Hamburger clown and ran with it?" Basil asked.

Neddy Not Donald scoffed, "Inspired. Hmph. He *stole* the idea. Not Donald's business took off like a rocket. Of course, it was going to work in Albuquerque! More traffic, more people, more money!"

"How do you know all this?" Meshy asked.

"I'm the original Neddy Not Donald," he said and shuffled off to greet a truck driver who just walked in.

"Is it me or is that clown creepy as hell?" Addy asked.

"Oh, he's creepy alright," Paloma said.

Meshy got excited, "Oh yeah, you picking something up from him?"

Paloma shook her head, "No, he's a withered old man still dressing up as a clown. You don't need to be a psychic to detect that from a mile away."

"Do you think he was telling the truth or he's going senile?" Bucky asked.

Meshy shrugged, "I dunno if the story holds weight but it's the best story for television."

Addy was surprised, "I thought you were supposed to be finding answers, not getting the best story?"

Meshy shrugged, "I'm trying to sell a television show, sometimes the truth needs a little help."

Basil added, "Well, it's all theoretical. I still say we need more research. There's got to be more information out there."

Meshy clapped Basil on the back, "You're right, skeptic. Let's start with researching the history of hamburger clowns."

Basil groaned but he loved the work. He was as curious about the old clown guy's story as the rest of the crew. Meshy told Bucky to get some shots of the old Neddy Not Donald for B-roll. Whether his story panned out or not, they could use some live-action clips of a hamburger clown as a person of interest.

"We've still got plenty of time before it starts getting dark. Basil, let's find the San Jon public library and comb through some records. Ain't much else we can do until dusk anyway."

They all agreed, hoping the San Jon Public Library would also provide some free air to rescue them from the remainder of the afternoon sun.

They all piled out into the heat of the New Mexican afternoon. They got into their respective vehicles to get the A/C blowing as fast as possible. Paloma hesitated getting into the van. She spotted the two guys in the desert watching them from the gas station across the road.

She elected not to raise the alarm. For now.

17

BUCKY COULDN'T UNDERSTAND why Paloma kept telling him to be quiet. Sure, they were in a library but they were the only ones in the library. He could tell because the San Jon Public Library was nothing but a rectangular brick building with four walls. The walls were lined with bookshelves and six round tables were scattered around the center of the space. There weren't any aisles. You could pirouette and see the entire catalog on display.

The librarian that sat at a drafting desk near the front door, didn't seem to mind that Bucky got excited about certain books that popped out at him from the shelves as he scanned the titles on the spines. She looked happy just to see people in the library.

Basil slammed another index card drawer closed. He must've been getting frustrated because each time he closed another draw, he slammed it louder than the previous. The last one he even said, "Shoot," louder than what would have been tolerated at a more frequently visited library.

Meshy didn't seem to mind. He was scanning the occult section. The occult section, Dewey decimal classification 133, only contained a dozen books. To Meshy they looked like a set of encyclopedias.

Paloma sat at one of the round tables, touching up her make-up and adjusting her hair. She didn't take off her bug-eyed sunglasses.

Addy sat by Paloma. She was checking her emails. They were more personal than business. The commercial real estate market in eastern New Mexico was drying up. It sounded like bad news but Addy saw a slow market as a way to try to move her older listings. A slow market meant limited stock and any buyers (there were always buyers) would have to buy the less desirable properties if they wanted to do business. Properties like Hamburger House.

She made the deal with Not Normal Investigations in haste. She wasn't sure she'd made the right decision bringing them in on the job. She thought she was doing it to prove to herself there were no ghosts and that she was going crazy. Spending the day with the investigation team, she had to admit, even if they didn't prove any paranormal activity, the show they were putting on might draw the right kind of attention.

"Paloma, how long do you think it will take for Hamburger House to air on television?" Addy asked.

Paloma shrugged, "Meshy has a contract, but until he delivers a whole season of episodes, there's no telling when it will get on TV. Or, *if*, it gets on TV. This television stuff, it's a tough game."

Addy was crestfallen, "You mean there's a chance this won't ever get on TV at all?"

"Look at me, darling. I'm camera-ready at all times. You don't think I've run the gamut of productions? I've shot three different reality dating shows. One game show. I hosted a cooking competition and did color commentary for some kind of college robot boxing tournament where I had to wear less than a bikini," Paloma shoved her ample bust out for Addy to admire, "If these two girls can't get a show greenlit, what can? Yeah, it isn't easy to break into TV."

"So, you're not a psychic? Not really?"

Paloma removed her glasses. Her hazel-green eyes grabbed Addy's attention. They didn't just see you. They saw *into* you. It was remarkable.

"I may be a lot of things, but a fraud is not one of them. Yes, I am slumming it with this crew just to get a gig on TV. But I know I'm made for the screen. And you don't get on TV by faking it. I can commune with the spirit world. That ain't no joke."

Addy believed her. It was hard not to with eyes that could see more than just what was in front of them. "What's it like?"

"Being psychic?"

"Yeah."

Paloma put her bug-eyed sunglasses back on, "Well, it's a bitch. Everyone thinks you're full of shit. Most everyone is like Basil, non-believers. I've learned to associate with folks like Meshy. On the outside, you would ask yourself why a girl like me hangs around a guy like him? On the inside, we're more alike than we appear. He gets me, and I feel like part of something instead of an outcast."

Addy felt bad for Paloma. All this time she looked at her and felt like she was a grade-A bitch. And, maybe she was a cold bitch who was too hot for her own good. She wasn't stone cold because she felt better than the rest, she was isolated from the rest of the world. All because of this ability she believed she possessed.

"Do you think there are spirits at Hamburger House?"

"If there are," Paloma said, as she resumed preening herself, "they're too afraid to talk to me, like everyone else." She ran lipstick across her plump lips, smacked them, and added, "Everyone, except for you Addy. And I was starting to think you were another cold bitch."

Paloma tipped her sunglasses down for a brief moment and shot Addy a wink. Addy chuckled.

The other boys all looked at them. When the girls huddled up and started giggling, trouble was sure to follow.

18

BASIL WAS FRUSTRATED. The San Jon Public Library had nothing on local history and even less about Hamburger House. The library was smaller than he expected, little more than a satellite of the Quay County library over in Tucumcari.

He had one, last-ditch effort in his research toolbox. The librarian.

He approached the woman sitting at the high-top desk. She was quiet, but regarded their group with the excitement of a child watching animals she'd never seen before at the zoo. Most librarians, he found, were closer to the stereotypical hair-in-a-ponytail, nerd glasses, and a modest sweater variety. No doubt the San Jon librarian was fresh out of college, eager to help the world with its referential needs. The indifferent world had not yet been able to sink its fangs into her and drain the eagerness from her soul.

"Hi," Basil offered with a big smile.

The librarian blew up like a balloon with excitement, she was going to have the opportunity to help a patron, "Hi! Can I help you find something?"

"Yes, actually, you can. Or, at least I hope you can. I know my way around libraries pretty well, but I can't seem to find what I'm looking for here."

"Oh, okay," the librarian tittered with nervous energy. She was going to be able to show off everything she'd learned in school. "What is it you're looking for?"

"Local history. Hamburger House out in Bard to be exact."

Basil expected the young librarian to deflate. Instead, she just about burst and leapt off her stool.

"Oh my gosh! My granny used to work there! How exciting," the librarian furrowed her eyebrows, "but, why would you want to research that old dump anyway? Kinda weird."

"Oh, my friends and I, we're shooting a documentary on the place. We were hoping to find out some history that we could relate to for the show. Especially anything on a clown that used to work there."

The librarian was beaming, "Crumbles Calhoun! Wow, so exciting!"

The librarian dragged Basil over to the closest table and sat him down. She flattened her skirt and sat next to him, holding his hands. She jittered, excited, "Granny used to tell me about Crumbles. She loved him."

This wasn't the type of reference material Basil was expecting to pull from but he was happy to take it. The librarian, introduced herself as Anna (or Anna Banana as her Granny always called her), and told Basil all the stories her Granny recollected to her over the years. Seems Granny and Crumbles Calhoun liked going to the sock hops at San Jon High and shared egg creams at Federici's Soda Parlor in Tucumcari. And, of course, the scandalous rendezvous necking out behind Hamburger House in the evenings after the dinner rush.

Grandma had told Anna Banana all kinds of stories about working at Hamburger House. It must have been the greatest time in Granny's life the way Anna recounted the stories passed down to her. Basil was getting bored with Anna's endless babble (had she taken a breath at all the whole time?) When she started talking about a rivalry between Crumbles and a new clown out in Albuquerque.

Basil perked up. He paused Anna Banana and gathered everyone else around. They were all going to want to hear this part.

Once everyone had gathered around the table, Anna continued, "So, anyway, there was this unsettling customer who Granny said always gave her the creeps."

The NNI crew exchanged glances.

Anna continued, "He'd be in everyday, order a cheeseburger and fries and he would just sit there and watch Granny and everyone else. And, once Crumbles went out roadside just before dinner to wave the customers into the lot, the guy wouldn't take his eyes off Crumbles for even a second. He stayed in his seat, well after he finished his meal, watching and jotting down notes in a pad he kept tucked inside his jacket.

"And after a few weeks of that, day after day, do you know what that creepy man did?"

"He dressed up like a clown and started doing the same thing at his own burger stand out in Albuquerque," Meshy said.

Anna Banana smiled, amazed that he knew, "Say, that's right. How'd you know?"

"We've been doing research," Basil said, "like I told you."

"Then you must know about what happened to Crumbles after that scoundrel did what he did?"

More glances around the table, "No," Meshy said, "We don't know much more about the story after that."

"I'm not surprised. Nobody talks much about what happened to Crumbles after that. It took me years to get Granny to talk about it. She wouldn't tell me either, not until she was sick and knew she wasn't going to be around much longer."

Anna Banana's cheery smile turned upside down thinking about her Granny, lying on her deathbed, "It was awful, she said. That's why nobody ever spoke about it. But someone needed to know the truth before she took it with her to the grave. So, she told me, and she passed the next day."

Addy took hold of Anna's hand, "What happened Anna?"

"Crumbles went mad," Anna said, looking down at the floor.

Meshy sprang to his feet, he looked mortified. "We should have been getting all this! Ma'am, would you mind repeating all that. For our research?"

Anna looked confused, but being the polite woman, her mother raised her to be, she agreed to help the strangers with their request. As long as it was research. This story wasn't meant to be gossip. That's why grandma kept it hush, hush for so long.

"Bucky. Camera. Now. We just scored us another segment," Meshy said, too excited, "for our, uhm, research project, that is."

19

DUSK COLLECTED light from the gravel parking lot at Hamburger House. The Not Normal Investigations crew were setting up inside for their next segment. The investigation of a portrait of a clown was next on the docket.

Addison waited outside. She'd become comfortable with Meshy, Basil and Paloma. And, almost too comfortable with Bucky. She wished she could steal another moment alone with him. She felt wicked the way she played with his emotions. He was smitten with her. She was certain. But, she also wanted some company. The sun was falling like an old balloon behind the distant horizon. It wasn't dark yet but she worried this place would be as creepy outside as it was inside come nightfall.

The story about Crumbles Calhoun didn't help settle her nerves. Crumbles sounded like the type of angry she felt when she experienced... activity.

This place is not haunted. This place is not haunted.

The more she thought about it, the less convinced she became. She wanted whatever was going on to stop. She wanted Meshy and his friends to make it go away. But, as the day wore on, she had the feeling that whatever was chained to Hamburger House was as much a part of its fabric as the brick and mortar. The ghosts *are* Hamburger House.

She'd never be able to sell the place. And the two guys that'd been watching them all day. They were back out at their post across the desert. Still watching. They knew. Word would get around fast. Hamburger House is cursed property. Do not buy!

She should've taken the loss. She could write this place off on her taxes. Failed investment or something like that. But no, she had to call in the ghostbusters and draw unwanted attention. It was a wash now, even if they were somehow able to rid the place of spirits.

Addison kicked some gravel and shuffled to the edge of Route 66. She imagined she was standing where Crumbles once stood. She saw the ghosts of Town & Country station wagons, bulbous Dodge Coronets, and sleek Plymouth Furies zipping past. She saw the excited faces of little children, noses pressed to the glass, waving wildly at Crumbles as he waved back.

She bet Crumbles didn't just wave at the cars in general. Crumbles was the type of clown that zeroed in on those kids' faces. He waved to each one personally. That's what made them go nuts. That's what made parents turn their cars around a quarter mile down the road and head back for lunch and dinner at Hamburger House. Crumbles cared about people.

It wasn't playing out in her mind. She saw it with her eyes, like a movie playing against a white fence. There, but not there. She blinked and shook her head.

She'd really zoned out for a moment. Did she just imagine all that, daydreaming after hearing Anna Banana's stories about Crumbles and her Granny? She felt odd, not herself, not real. What was happening?

She stepped away from the edge of the highway. The world around her became sharper. It was like she had stepped out of a frosted glass booth. The crispness of reality came back into focus.

Addison hugged herself. Chills ran through her body. She may have experienced another... event. But she was outside.

She wasn't safe anywhere anymore. She turned and walked as fast as her heels would allow her and went inside Hamburger House.

20

Meshy stood to the left of the portrait of Crumbles the Clown. He stood with his hands shoved into his pockets, his investigation stance. A device that looked like an old-time transistor radio sat on a table under the picture. There were wires tangled around the front of the speaker, lit up with several white LED lights. A telescoping antenna protruded from the top. The box was producing a lot of annoying chatter like it was shuffling through radio channels at a manic rate.

"Can you tell us your name?" Meshy asked aloud.

More disturbing radio noises.

"Are you the clown in this picture I'm standing next to?"

Indiscernible noise.

"There are some items I've placed around me that you can interact with. If you touch them, they will light up. Can you touch one of those eggs on the floor and make it light up so we know you're here?"

The rest of the team waited for any type of interaction. They had the usual array of gadgets deployed: motion sensors, temperature gauges, and the Yes/No eggs. They fired up the Geoport, the radio making the irritating sounds. It was supposed to allow vocal interaction with the spirits. Meshy had tried to explain to the rest of the team how it worked but it didn't make sense to any of them.

Basil figured it was picking up stray AM radio signals. It was probably constructed to scan through the channels so fast that, unless it picked up a really strong frequency, it spat out mostly garbled gibberish. But if it hit a strong wave, a word or two might come across the nonsense and sound like a ghost was talking. Paloma and Bucky believed it was ghosts talking, they'd seen enough crazy shit to think otherwise.

"You don't need to be scared of us. We just want to talk to you. We want to hear about you and the clown from Albuquerque. Can you tell us about that?"

The temperature meter lit up. The needle pinned itself.

"You've got a cold spot Meshy," Paloma announced.

"Whoa!" Meshy said, excited about the hit. "Is that you? Crumbles? Can you tell us your name?"

Meshy wanted a vocalization from the GeoPort. That device alone brought ghost hunting out of the Middle Ages. If they could get verbal interaction with the spirits in Hamburger House, they had a show. Hell, he'd have a lock on selling the series to a streaming service.

More scrambled radio garble then, "Ko."

"Ko!" Meshy almost jumped.

"I heard it." Paloma said.

"Ko, are you the fry cook?"

The 'Yes' egg twinkled. Meshy was giddy. They were getting some action.

"Ko, were you murdered by the clown in this picture next to me?"

"Get out!" A voice, deep and stern, shot out of the GeoPort.

"Whoa, it doesn't want us here." Meshy said, stating the obvious. "That wasn't Ko's voice."

"It was different. Deeper." Paloma confirmed.

"Ko, is there another spirit here with you? Is Crumbles here? Was that you Crumbles? Do you not want us here?"

Meshy tensed up. He felt like someone turned on the air, full blast. He was cold.

"It just got cold here where I'm standing. Are you cold?" he asked Paloma.

Paloma stood about six feet away from where Meshy was. She said she didn't feel anything.

"Hey!" the camera jolted when Bucky spun. He'd been poked hard in the neck. "Wow, something just jabbed me in the neck."

"Crumbles? Did you just poke Bucky? Are you angry that we're here?"

"Leave." came the softer male voice first heard from the GeoPort.

"You want us to leave? We can't leave. We want to hear your story. Why are you angry with us?"

Both the 'Yes' and 'No' eggs lit up at the same time.

Paloma took a step back from all the activity. She'd never experienced this level of interaction. She should've been picking up something or someone with this much going on and still she felt nothing. Things weren't making much sense on this investigation.

"Ko, do you want us to come talk to you over by the fryolator?" Meshy asked.

'No' egg twinkled.

"No? You want us to stay here?"

"Yas." came the voice among the radio garble.

"Was that a yes? Did you say yes?"

The cold rushed away from around Meshy. "It's gone. The cold. It just snapped back to normal temperature. Were we picking up anything on the thermal meter?"

Paloma said she wasn't sure. She'd lost focus monitoring the meters. She was more concerned about her abilities being shut down.

"Paloma, can you reach out and see if Ko wants to talk to you?"

Paloma nodded. The cameras were rolling. No time for a crisis. She took off her bug-eyed sunglasses, her signature moves for the cameras. It meant she was going into psychic mode. A visual queue she created. In truth, she couldn't turn her abilities on and off like a switch. They were ever present, like breathing. She rolled her eyes into the back of her head and cast her arms out wide. Another theatrical motion, meaningless to her actual ability.

Through the fuzz, she did feel a presence. "There is something here. Faint. Very faint."

"Can you sense what it is? Male, female?" Meshy asked. Bucky had the camera locked on Paloma.

"It... it is a being. I sense its presence. Not communicative. Hiding. It's hiding from me."

Wow. Paloma was able to focus. She was picking up a presence. Whenever she was able to hone in on a spirit, it usually came forward. Like she cast an invitation. This energy she felt, it resisted her. It was hard to describe. But she felt shunned.

"It... it won't come forward."

"Why won't you talk to Paloma? She's harmless. You can tell her anything. She can't hurt you. You can talk through her and tell her anything and she'll repeat what you tell her. You can even tell her not to say anything. Talk to her," Meshy begged.

The activity quieted down as rapidly as it escalated. The meters fell static, no lights twinkled and the GeoPort was all radio noise again.

They heard the door open. Addison ran in. She looked like she'd just seen a ghost.

Meshy looked at Bucky, "Cut," he commanded.

Bucky stopped rolling. He set the camera down and rubbed the back of his neck. It still smarted. Whatever jabbed his neck sure felt real.

21

ADDISON RAN TO BUCKY. Bucky hugged her with his free arm. He dared not put the camera down to fully embrace her.

Addy was huffing and puffing like she'd run clear across New Mexico, "Something happened outside."

"Was it those two guys?" Paloma asked.

Addy shook her head no, "I saw something. Like I was transported."

Meshy rushed to her side, "Visions? You had visions?"

Addy caught her breath, "Sorta. It's hard to describe."

"Take your time," Meshy assured her, pulling her away from Bucky and leading her to sit down at one of the booths. "Explain exactly what happened?" he asked, motioning for Bucky to start recording.

Addison placed her hand across her eyes and looked at the ground. She was playing it over in her head, "I just wanted to walk to the side of the highway, like we heard the clown used to do. I dunno, just to feel what it might have been like. As I stood there, I saw cars, old cars, start to pass by. They were there, but they weren't. I saw boys and girls waving at me. I saw their faces. It was like when you think a dream is so real when you first wake up. Like, it actually happened. I was there."

Paloma took her hand, "You *were* there."

Addy looked at Paloma, confused.

"There's energy out there. You were drawn to it. Enveloped by it."

"You saw what Crumbles saw, Addy!" Meshy was too excited. "We've got psychic activity!" Meshy looked at the camera, narrating, "What we've just experienced was coincidental psychic activity. Paloma picks up on the activity, feeling shoved away from it. But now we know that's because Addy was interacting with it. Wow!"

Paloma didn't say anything, not while the camera was rolling. But, Meshy had it wrong. What happened to Addy was a psychic event but it was a connection with the past, like she walked into a movie that was already playing. Paloma was interacting with something in the now. She still felt it, hiding.

She reached out, silent. It cowered from her. It wasn't scared. It was... unsure.

Meshy continued to get Addy to recount her experience. Addy talked a bit more but was short on answers when she realized the camera was recording her.

"Can you just get rid of this thing? Now. Please?" She asked Bucky, not Meshy.

Bucky looked at Meshy, "Can't we do something Meshy?"

"I need one more segment. We're so close to capturing something big here," Meshy almost had a show. He couldn't go chasing ghosts away now. "Addy, do you want to wait outside?"

"No, no. I don't want to be alone. I'll be okay here. Or, better than I would be out there. Please, hurry. And, don't let them do anything freaky."

The only thing Meshy wanted the ghosts of Hamburger House to do was something freaky. "Just stick behind Bucky and stay out of frame. You'll be fine," he assured Addy, "I want to set up in front of the cash registers. I want to get right between these two spirits. Let's see if we can't get them to hash this out."

Meshy had a game plan. It was time to pull out all the stops. There were two spirits here and neither liked the other. He was going to facilitate a battle. If Addy wanted the ghosts gone, maybe the way to do that was to get them to have a paranormal rumble.

And Meshy was going to capture it all on camera.

22

"BUCKY, GET THE SLS," Meshy ordered.

Bucky dashed to the arsenal of equipment stacked near the door. He retrieved a black, hard-shell briefcase and set it down on one of the tabletops. He clicked open the clasps and lifted the lid. Inside, cradled in preformed foam rubber was a tiny camera that looked like a bastard sports camera. Next to it, another device that looked something like a standard computer tablet, but with an array of physical buttons along one of the short sides. The SLS camera.

Bucky got to work mounting the camera on a tripod. He ran some cables between the camera and the tablet device which he mounted on an adjacent tripod. Addy watched with rapt attention.

"What's this SLS camera do?" Addy asked.

"It sees ghosts," Bucky said.

Addy didn't like the sound of that. Her mind wouldn't be able to handle seeing a ghost. She could rationalize away odd sounds and anomalies. But seeing a ghost? Nope. She wouldn't be able to unsee it and thus wouldn't be able to convince herself she didn't see one.

"I'll pass."

"This means you're going back outside again?" Bucky sounded disappointed.

Addy hated to break his heart but, yeah, she thought she might go outside again. She walked over to Basil, who was still pouring over data on his phone.

"Can you step outside with me? I need some air." Addy asked Basil.

Basil scrolled another page then took his eyes off the screen to look at Addy, "Sure. Sure. I don't need to be around while they set up. I do have to be on set when they start shooting again though."

She'd take it, "That's fine."

They walked outside. Addy dug into her purse and pulled out a container of minty gum. She offered a piece to Basil who declined, then shook one out into her hand and popped it in her mouth. She hadn't realized how her mouth had soured until the icy cool peppermint released from the shell of gum. A sure sign her nerves were churning her guts below.

Basil leaned against the building, one foot up against the faux adobe stucco. "Not finding much about the clown wars. The only thing strange that seems to happen around here are UFOs."

Addy chuckled a bit, "Roswell gets into everyone's head around here. You know that."

Basil nodded, "Yeah, but Roswell is like three hours from here."

"Everything is three hours from here. The desert is deserted. It attracts UFOs."

It wasn't just Roswell that brought constant stories of UFOs. The desert was the perfect place for covert government operations, both land and air-based. You could hide a lot more than bodies out in the desert. New Mexicans understood UFO activity to coincide with government testing of one kind or another. It was the tourists who believed the activity was connected to little green men.

"Maybe Bard could be the new Roswell," she mused. It's something residents would say whenever UFOs made it into local news.

"Maybe if you're lucky, they'll land at Hamburger House for a bite to eat and you could turn the place into another alien gift shop."

There was that idea again. Forget selling Hamburger House as a restaurant. Embrace its abnormalities and sell it as a haunted attraction or, Heaven help her, the site of a UFO crash.

"Are you sure Meshy wouldn't want to buy this place? It could help with the branding. Think about it, Not Normal Investigations presents The Haunted Hamburger House experience. Assuming, of course, he can prove it's haunted."

"Oh, he'll prove it's haunted. To himself, anyway. Don't worry about that. It's convincing everyone else that it's haunted, that's the trick."

"What makes you say that?"

Basil took a deep breath. He looked around. All he saw were the two guys in the desert. He was pretty sure they couldn't hear him from where they were. And if they did, they weren't likely to repeat it back to Meshy. "Every place we investigate is haunted. That's the deal. Get it? If there ain't no ghosts, there ain't no show."

"Are you saying it's fake?"

"*I'm* saying it's fake, yes. But, that's my job. That's the angle. None of the other ghost investigators employ a skeptic on the team to debunk them on the spot. He's got a potential deal if he hires a skeptic and can still produce ghosts."

"So, it's fake and he's still finding ghosts?"

"Sorta. It's all in the gear. The gear is all real. The key is manipulating the story to frame the gear. That's why my secondary job is getting the story. Normally, we're investigating people's homes. They tend to know the history of their houses. This place, it's a different situation. The history is harder to hunt down since there isn't someone who has all the information. Hell, a lot of times, the family has already invented a story for the ghosts they believe haunt their house."

"Is that why Meshy quit after the first segment this afternoon? He captured the electricity turning itself on but he didn't have any story to tell about why it was doing that?"

Basil laughed, "We got so lucky running into that clown and then the librarian. Doesn't it seem like a coincidence to you? All the pieces fell into place while we were out to lunch."

Addy got so caught up in the spectacle of the story that she had to admit now, looking back on it, that it was all rather crazy coincidence. "Plants?"

Basil rubbed his chin, he'd been mulling the same question in his own mind, "Nah, I don't think so. There's a modicum of truth to it. The clown's story anyway. It lines up with what I've found. It's the librarian's story I'm not sure about. Local legend perhaps? This place used to be jumping a long time ago.

Addy shuddered. She looked at Route 66 and recalled her vivid daydream. It was jumping. Cars were *turning around* on the highway. People were drawn to this place.

People were drawn to this place...

She looked out across the desert. The two guys, still standing next to their van. Still vigilant. "And them," Addy said, "They're drawn to this place too. What do you make of them? Curious locals, like Meshy insists?"

"Could be. But, those two are some persistent locals. It is a one-horse town we're in. We might be exciting enough to keep 'em entertained all day. But the way they've been watching? Feels more like reconnaissance to me, though what for I have no idea. Could be people from the sheriff's office. So, in that way, still curious locals, I suppose."

Basil made Addy feel a lot better. He was rational, like her. He'd seen weird things too. He'd experienced far crazier shit than Addy had and yet he was cool and collected. He could explain most of it and whatever he couldn't he was sure he would figure out eventually.

This place is not haunted.

"I gotta get back inside. Looks like they're ready. Coming back in?"

Addy felt a lot better, "Nah, think I'll stay out and look for shooting stars for a bit."

Basil went back inside. Addison looked to the heavens and waited for a star to wish upon.

23

"THANKS FOR JOINING US, CASANOVA," Meshy said to Basil.

"The lady asked me to join her. Should I not be a gentleman?"

"You're on the clock," Meshy said.

Basil took up position, near Paloma.

Meshy stood in front of the cash register where the ghostwriting appeared in the dust. He'd already had Bucky take some stills of the writing, 'Get Out' to add in during post-production. Still shots were boring but with the right voiceover narrative, they could send chills down the viewer's spines. People who watched ghost shows were ready to believe if you gave them a good story.

All their gadgets were set up on the counter: meters, gauges, lights, sensors, and audio feedback devices. Two cameras were rolling, the handheld and the SLS. Meshy was going to capture everything.

Paloma stood out of frame with Basil alongside. A quick pan to Bucky's right and he could grab reaction shots without cutting. They could clean it all up in post-production. The key was to get everything without missing a beat.

"Okay, Bucky. Roll!" Meshy announced and the ghost investigator veneer washed over his face. "We're standing near the cash register," He called out to whatever ghosts were listening inside Hamburger House, "you told the lady who comes here to get out. You wrote that in the dust next to this register. Do you remember doing that?"

They listened. The GeoPort spit out garbled chatter. The other gadgets remained static.

"Why do you get angry when people visit here?"

Two, harsh, deep words garbled out of the GeoPort.

"Get out? Did you just say get out?" Later, in post-production, they would inject a quick replay of the audio. It would still sound deep and mumbled like it was underwater but with a little coaxing from some subtitles, they could lead viewers at home to believe the words were, "Get out."

"Why do you want us to leave?"

The 'Yes' egg twinkled. Meshy pointed at it, "Yes? Yes, you want us to leave? Don't you want to tell us your story?"

There was almost zero reaction, but then the 'No' egg twinkled.

Another voice blurted out of the GeoPort. The word was short, indecipherable, and spoken in less of a baritone. In post-production, the replay would suggest the name, "Ko" was uttered.

Meshy looked to Paloma, "Did it just say Ko?"

Bucky panned slightly right, Paloma came into frame, "Maybe Ko, yes." she said. "I'm getting something else though."

Bucky started to pan back to a single shot of Meshy but stuttered and held Paloma in frame with him. "I think it's trying to tell me to go away. That energy that was hiding from me. I think it's asking us to leave it alone."

"That's Paloma," Meshy called out to the spirits, "Are you finding it easier to communicate with her? She doesn't want to go away. She wants to listen to you."

"Ss'hole," a deep growl came out of the GeoPort. Later, in post-production there would be some argument as to whether they could subtitle the word 'asshole' on screen and still get played on a family cable channel.

Before Meshy could react, Paloma said, "It asked if I know this guy is an asshole?"

Meshy gasped. It wasn't because Paloma was communicating with the spirits. He was worried they'd have to edit that out because she said asshole.

He pushed forward, "You don't like me? You don't have to talk to me. You can talk through Paloma. Or you can use the GeoPort. Just talk. We can hear you."

"Ruined." the GeoPort said in its deep voice. That was clear, no need for subtitles.

"Get out," the GeoPort announced but in another voice, "Go away."

Meshy's mouth was a big O. "I've never heard this before. We're picking up a conversation between two spirits.

"You're picking up two radio stations," Basil said, doing his job as a skeptic at the exact wrong time.

"Basil, you can be so narrow-minded. Never in the history of ghost investigations has anyone recorded spirit interaction. You just heard something captured for the very first time and you want to dismiss it?"

"The GeoPort picks up radio waves. It's the most likely explanation."

"I'm mapping something," Bucky called out from behind the camera. He pointed to the SLS camera display.

Between Meshy and Paloma, a digitized stick figure appeared. It was directly in front of the counter where 'Get Out' was written in dust. The stick figure had no head. The SLS camera didn't map out a head but it was mapping out something vaguely humanoid. In the shot, Meshy and Paloma were also mapped out, the camera mapped out anything it thought represented a body whether you could see it or not.

"Oh, I see it," Meshy said. "Do you see that Paloma?"

Paloma, nor Basil, could see the SLS display from the angle they were standing at. Meshy had to relay what he was seeing.

"It's right next to you, in front of the dust writing."

Paloma reached out. On the SLS display, the invisible figure stepped away from Paloma's hand. "Oh wow, it just moved away from your hand. It seems to be a bit frightened. I don't want to reach out or it might go away.

"Is that you Crumbles? Paloma won't touch you."

"Ko." the GeoPort announced in a friendlier voice.

The needle on the thermal meter danced out of the corner of Meshy's eye. "Cold spot."

Everything was happening at once. Meters were spiking, lights were twinkling and the GeoPort was talking like an excited three-year-old child. And to top it off, they were mapping an entity and it was interacting with them. This was a ghost investigator's wet dream! Meshy was so excited he didn't know what to do next. Spirits were picky and if you freaked them out or pissed them off, they'd leave as quickly as they made themselves known. Or worse, they could become agitated and resort to possession.

Meshy didn't have to do anything. They were about to experience something out of this world.

24

ADDY FELT BETTER after talking to Basil. She was comfortable being outside on her own again. His skepticism was so matter-of-fact. She felt foolish for becoming swept up in all the Meshy was peddling.

This place is not haunted.

She said it to herself and believed it this time. She looked at the stars, now salting the clear New Mexican evening sky. A meteorite flashed across the panorama. Addy laughed. A shooting star, how perfect. Like the universe thanked her for coming back into sync with reality.

"Excuse me."

Addy spun at the sound of the man's voice. Two men actually. They'd snuck up behind her while she was stargazing.

"Where the hell did you come from," Addy asked, her eyes darting between the two individuals.

One of the men held his hands in front of him to show they meant no harm, "Easy. Sorry, we snuck up on you. We've been watching you all day."

Addy cut him off, "You're the two guys out in the desert?" she looked around, "Where's your van?"

"You are in danger. I need you to come with us," the guy said, ignoring Addy's question.

"Uhm, no. I'm not going anywhere with you. My friends are inside. You need to stay away from me."

"Miss, we really don't have time for this. You've caused enough problems as it is," He pointed inside, "bringing them here was a big mistake."

Addy took a step backward toward Hamburger House. She wasn't sure she could make up the distance to the front door in her shoes. Curse her professional appearance.

The second man, who hadn't said a word yet, produced a pistol. Addy gasped, they meant to take her by force if necessary. She had to risk running, it was her only hope. The gun kept her in place. She wasn't sure if they would really shoot her or not if she chose to run.

Addy did the only thing she could at that moment. She screamed.

The two men rushed her, "Grab her Number B!" the main guy said. He lunged at Addison and had her around the waist in a blink.

The other guy hesitated, "Don't use my name Number A!"

"B! Just help me." Number A had his hand over Addison's mouth now, muffling her screams.

Number B produced a handful of zip ties from his jacket as he wrestled Addison's hands together. She fought to keep herself from getting bound but Number A covered her nose, making it clear he would suffocate her if she kept resisting.

Number B was able to secure her hands without any further resistance. The two of them picked her up and carried her up the road to their van. They were glad the investigation team inside was preoccupied with their little show. Those people had no clue what they were messing with here.

25

THE FRYOLATOR TURNED itself back on. It buzzed and blinked the way it did years ago when Hamburger House was busy filling fast food orders for hungry kids and their parents. The GeoPort started broadcasting sizzling sounds.

Before Meshy had time to react to the new action, Paloma yelped and went down on one knee. She was holding her hands over her ears like she was hearing something too loud to handle.

Basil rushed to her side, "Are you okay? What's wrong?"

Paloma cried, "It's screaming, 'Help! Help!'"

Meshy called out to the ghosts, "Why are you doing this to Paloma? You're hurting her. She can't help you if you're hurting her! You need to stop!"

Paloma screamed in pain, she was sweating and straining to speak.

"Help her you idiots!" Meshy knelt down next to Paloma.

Basil looked him in the eyes, staring daggers. "What do you need me to do Paloma? I think we need to get her out of here."

Meshy turned and yelled at Bucky, "Don't you dare stop recording!"

Meshy and Basil helped Paloma to her feet. She grunted and said, "Not me. Not me. Her! Her! Her!"

Meshy looked at Basil, "What the hell is she talking about?"

Basil shouted back, "I don't know, you're the ghost whisperer, not me!"

Meshy curled his lip. He wanted to lay into Basil. This wasn't the time. They needed to help Paloma. He'd seen her channel spirits before but this was something her body couldn't handle. He was afraid she'd been possessed. That was outside the scope of his expertise.

Meshy and Basil lifted Paloma to her feet. They each draped one of her arms around their necks. Bucky kept shooting.

"Who do we need to help?" Meshy asked.

Paloma's head lolled back. "Thaaaaaa gurllllll." she said.

What kind of demon tells people to help someone out? This was weird, Meshy thought.

"Oh shit, Addy!" Basil said, "It's Addy!"

"Thaaaaaa gurllll."

"Addy?" Meshy asked.

"Thaaaa gurllll."

Paloma's head snapped upright again. The fryolator stopped buzzing and all their ghost detection devices went still.

"Addy?" Meshy asked Paloma again.

"Huh?" Paloma asked as if she just joined the conversation.

"Come on, we have to sit her down and go check on Addy. Something's not right." Basil kept looking outside, anxious, he didn't see Addy standing around in the parking lot.

Meshy and Basil helped Paloma over to one of the booths and sat her down. Meshy didn't know if he should keep the camera rolling on Paloma or send Bucky out with Basil to look for Addy.

"Bucky. Just, stay here. Stay with Paloma. Stop recording for now. But, damnit, don't put that camera down whatever you do. At the first sign of anything you start recording again. I'm going out with Basil to check on Addy."

"She's taken." Paloma said, catching her breath.

"Taken? What do you mean?" Meshy asked.

"I don't know what I mean. I just remember seeing her taken."

"Let's go." Basil urged Meshy, already making his way to the door.

Meshy ran out behind Basil. Basil stood still in the middle of the lot. Out on Route 66, right in front of Hamburger House, a van idled.

"Is that the van those two guys were in?" Meshy asked.

"I think so." Basil started walking toward the van.

"Wait," Meshy said, grabbing him by the shoulder, "What if they take us too?"

"Better us than Addy," Basil said, shrugging Meshy's hand off his shoulder.

Meshy rushed to keep up with Basil. He didn't think this was a good idea at all.

"Besides," Basil said and giggled, "they're probably just fans or curious locals, right Meshy?"

They got to the side of the van. Nobody sat in the driver's seat. The engine was still running. Basil tilted his head toward the back of the van. Meshy moved that way, Basil right behind him.

They stood in front of the two back doors of the black van. No windows to look inside. No handle to pop it open, just a keyed lock. Basil leaned in to knock.

Both doors pushed open. They were greeted by two guys dressed in black suits and wearing black masks that covered everything but their eyes. They each held an odd-looking pistol aimed at the ghost investigators. Behind them, tied to a chair, was Addy.

"Which one of you is the psychic?" one of the masked men asked.

26

"GEEZ, PALOMA, WHAT WAS THAT?" Bucky asked. He'd captured some odd stuff on camera but never anything like that.

"I don't know. I..." Paloma trailed off, trying to find the words for what she experienced, "That wasn't a spirit. It wasn't a demon. Something else entered my mind. It felt like someone walked inside of me. It was crazy. You said I was screaming something about helping her?"

"Yeah. Addy."

"I don't know what I said. I felt frozen. I saw these images. A van. Two men. Like I was watching television. It was here but it was from a different vantage point. A long shot, not from inside and not in the parking lot. But it was definitely here."

"That's crazy. How do you feel? Your color is starting to come back."

"Better. I could use water. I'm parched."

"There's water out in the van. Want me to go get one? I could see if they found Addy yet."

"I'll go with you."

"Ya sure?"

"Bucky, you don't think I'm gonna let some punk ass ghost hold me back, do you?"

Bucky laughed. Paloma didn't take shit from anyone, living or dead. He extended a hand to help her up. Her head wasn't swimming any more. She was ready to take on the world again, and she wanted to figure out what that odd vision was about. It had to have been the two men in the desert that she'd been keeping a close eye on all day. She knew they weren't to be trusted.

Bucky and Paloma walked outside. Bucky brought the camera with him. He didn't want to get in trouble with Meshy again. Sure enough, they saw Basil and Meshy standing behind the black van, its back door opened. Neither of them was able to see who was in the van. Paloma was sure it was the two guys across the desert, and she was pretty sure the two guys had guns or else Basil and Meshy wouldn't have had their hands raised in the air.

"What the fu—" Bucky started to ask before Paloma slapped her hand over his mouth.

"Shh." She demanded in a whisper.

Paloma assessed the situation. She could see Basil and Meshy were talking. There was some back and forth going on, seemed nothing rash was about to happen. But time was precious if guns were involved.

She noted nobody in the front of the van. If Bucky and she could manage to get to the front of the vehicle, they could create a diversion and the other two could make a break for it. To where, she wasn't sure but if they could get some cover that would be better than nothing.

She whispered her plan to Bucky. Bucky didn't like the idea of being bait but he understood what Paloma was going for. He trusted her. He knew what to do and he repeated the steps back to be sure he got it.

"Let's go."

Paloma crept up to the front of the van. There were no windows in the back, as long as nobody poked their head out, they wouldn't see her. Bucky walked toward the open doors on the back. His aim was to walk past Basil and Meshy like nothing was happening.

If he looked out of place and dumb enough, it would create just enough of a diversion for Paloma to jump in the driver seat and take control the van.

As he approached the back of the van, he realized Paloma had forgotten one thing. Addy. Oh shit! What if Addy was in the back of that van. If they sounded the alarm and the van took off, they'd lose her forever.

He stopped. He couldn't go through with the plan. What if Addy got killed? They couldn't do this. He looked at Paloma. He wanted to signal to her to stop but Paloma had frozen too.

She was a ghost.

Instead of warning her, he started recording her.

27

NUMBER A AIMED his pistol at Addy's head. "The Psychic, now, or else."

The pistol was the oddest-looking gun Meshy had ever seen. The barrel was a bit egg shaped. It had fins along its sides and the tip of the gun tapered off into a thin point with a silver ball on the end. It looked a bit like a cheesy ray gun you'd see in old black and white sci-fi movies.

"Is that a toy gun?" Meshy said. It looked too ridiculous to be menacing, he decided.

Number B laughed, "He thinks the Parsatron-500 is a toy!" Number B aimed his pistol at Meshy and Basil. Before they could cringe, he pulled off a shot that sent a blur of light slashing between the two men.

Basil and Meshy looked over their shoulders. Nothing blew up or exploded or went bang.

"What was that?" Meshy asked.

"Told ya it wasn't a toy." Number B said and laughed again.

"Enough! You know we have to file a report every time you fire that thing off Number B. What the hell is wrong with you?" Number A yelled.

"Guys," Basil asked, also thinking they were being put on, "What's going on here?"

"We need the psychic." Number A said, training his Parsatron-500 on Meshy again.

"Well, she's not the psychic," Meshy said, indicating Addy.

"We've figured that out, pal." Number B said.

"You're not going to find any psychics here. Or anywhere. They aren't real, you know?" Basil said, and meant it.

"Look," Number A pointed the gun at Basil now, "Our report says there's a psychic on your team. Most likely the female. This female ain't the one so where's the leggy woman?"

"She's not a psychic." Basil insisted.

Meshy buttoned his lip. He knew he couldn't say it and believe it like Basil. For once, he thought, it just might pay off having a skeptic on this team. Meshy scanned the van with his eyes as the two guys argued a bit more about the existence of psychics with Basil. Behind Addy he could see a rack with devices and gadgets that looked a lot like ghost hunting equipment. They had lights and dials and meters and wires but otherwise didn't resemble any paranormal equipment he'd ever used before. There was also something that looked like a cage with a clear plastic capsule inside it.

Meshy thought these guys were ghost hunters as well. By the look of their gear, they weren't backyard hobbyists. Now he thought these guys were pissed Not Normal was stepping on their territory. And they were just stupid enough to think they could lure Paloma away to their team. They were trying to strong arm a deal.

"You guys are into some kinky shit," Meshy said, cutting off the heated discussion on the existence of psychics.

"Huh?" Number B asked.

Meshy nodded to the cage behind them, "You, ahh, into some of the S&M stuff? Got some whips and chains back there too? Maybe next to those fancy EVP's?"

He made sure he knew that they knew that he knew what they were up to. The two guys played dumb. Number A was embarrassed that Meshy suggested their van was some sort of rape kink van.

Number B got defensive, thinking Meshy was insinuating he and Number A were doing depraved things to one another in the back of the van.

Meshy was ready to call their bluff. The pistols were obviously props. These guys were obviously the competition and Addison was certainly in no danger. He was about to shove past the two guys and grab Addy out of the back of the van when he heard Bucky call out, "Meshy, ghost! We've got activity!"

Meshy turned to his left and saw Bucky holding the camera up, pointing toward the front of the van. Before he could move to get a look past the back door of the van, the two guys pounced, tackling Meshy and Basil to the ground.

28

CRUMBLES THE CLOWN stood at the edge of Route 66 and waited for the cars. None had come for a long, long time. Not the way they did before. The cars were precious now, like drops of water in the desert.

A car would pass by now and then. He'd wave but they didn't stop anymore. The faces of the children inside were older now. They didn't get excited over a clown. Not even a clown as happy as Crumbles.

Crumbles thought maybe the clown he left inside Hamburger House was too angry. He scared folks away. All the joy of a clown was sapped from him. Crumbles didn't like Angry Crumbles. That's why he left Angry Crumbles the Clown inside. He wanted to be outside, by the road. He wanted to wave and invite the kids in for a bite to eat on their way to the Golden Coast. He loved to be a cheerful recollection on the road of happy memories.

But the cars barely came. They never stopped. And, on those rare, joyous moments when a car or two would pull in the parking lot and visit, Angry Crumbles would scare them away.

It was hard to be a happy clown when you were sad. Crumbles was a professional though. He'd sigh, take a deep breath, and smile to make his painted-on face big and happy once again. He'd wait, practicing his inviting wave.

Now there were visitors. They'd stayed all day. They didn't seem bothered by the angry Crumbles inside. They were curious about him. Crumbles liked that. He thought maybe angry Crumbles needed someone to talk about his feelings with. He had a lot of baggage and held a ball of anger inside for a long, long time.

And now, there were other visitors. They stopped, but didn't pull into the parking lot. They weren't happy. They left their van on the side of the highway and they were taking his happy customers away.

Crumbles wasn't content with that. Hope was so close. He wanted to chase away the angry people, inside and out. But he was stuck where he was. His whole being was here, at the side of Route 66, waving at children and their parents, inviting them in.

Oh, if only he could move. He'd walk right over to those two men who were *stealing his customers* and he would teach them a lesson. He'd show them what happens when you make Crumbles angry, angry like Angry Crumbles. Then they might change their minds about stopping in for a burger, fries and a smile.

Then, the woman inhabited his space. Another vessel, like the other woman, earlier. But this woman was even better. She was a vessel. He could wear her, like a clown jumper.

Crumbles struggled with the phantom weight of his new body. It had been a long time since he'd felt tangible. He staggered a bit, like he was drunk. He turned and wobbled on his feet. He wasn't used to wearing heels. He saw a man, pointing a camera at him, and he looked surprised to see Crumbles.

It had been a long, long time since anyone had *seen* Crumbles. He'd wave and wave but the kids didn't wave back. Their parents didn't point and smile. They looked through him, like he wasn't there.

The man had his camera trained on Crumbles. It felt wonderful to be noticed after all this time. The cameraman was acting as if he'd never seen a clown before in his life. What a wonderful gift, a clown.

Crumbles smiled and waved at the cameraman. Where was his

family, his children? Crumbles bowed and gestured toward Hamburger House, inviting him inside for fun and a good meal at a reasonable price.

The cameraman kept filming him.

Crumbles was going to honk his big red nose for the camera but another man, holding a gun, charged the cameraman from behind the van on the side of the road. The cameraman went down. A woman ran after the attacker. She pounced on the two men.

There was no fighting at Hamburger House. This is a family establishment and fights wouldn't be tolerated. Crumbles grew angry like Angry Crumbles. He charged in to stop the fight. Not on his watch!

29

ADDISON WATCHED Number A and Number B pounce on Meshy and Basil. They'd become distracted by Bucky yelling about ghosts. He was so adorable but he could be a total butthead at times. Number A had Meshy down on the road, his face mashed into the blacktop. Basil was on his back, struggling to get out from under Number B.

Basil got an arm free and swung at Number B's face, connecting with his cheek. Number B countered by slamming the butt of his pistol against Basil's head. The skeptic stopped fighting.

Addison didn't know if he'd been knocked out or killed. She was stunned.

Number A, holding down Meshy, told Number B to go get Bucky.

Number B nodded, and dashed after Bucky.

That got Addison's attention. Her hands were bound but not her legs. She jumped out of the van, kicked Number A in the back of the head and ran after Number B who now had Bucky tackled down to the ground.

Addison didn't have a plan. She threw herself on top of Bucky and Number B. If nothing else, she hoped she'd distract Number B, giving Bucky a chance to get away from him. She landed on top of

Number B. She felt the two men wrestling underneath but didn't have use of her hands so she used her next best weapon, her mouth. Number B kept screaming as he rolled off Bucky. Addison went for the ride and was pinned underneath Number B.

Bucky dropped the camera. It lay on its side, still recording a close-up of Addison and Number B in frame. Since the shot was so tight, nobody could see the ghostly form of Paloma yank Number B off of Addison and sling him with an inhuman might out into the road. Number B came to a stop on the faded double yellow line in the middle of the road. He was going to have a nasty case of road rash in the morning.

The only portion of the action the camera captured was the side of Paloma's translucent leg as she stepped over Addy to help her get up. Contention over whether Paloma had become an actual apparition or if it was special effects foolery done in post-production would be debated by fans of the show in the years to come.

Before Bucky and Addy had a moment to breathe and ask Paloma why she was a ghost, they heard Meshy grunting, still struggling with Number A, and squirming like hell to get out from under his attacker.

Number A found his pistol lying on the road next to him. He grabbed it, and aimed it at the back of Meshy's head.

"No!" Addy called out.

"He's out on the road. I can't do anything," Paloma said but she sounded more like an old man than a feminine beauty.

"I better get the camera," Bucky said.

"What? No, Bucky, Jesus!" Addy said, exasperated with Bucky's one-track mind. She didn't blame him, she blamed Meshy for screwing up his priorities.

Meshy wriggled underneath Number A like an angry shark dragged onto the beach. Number A couldn't keep his strange pistol trained on Meshy. "Stop fighting. Don't make this any harder than it has to be." they could hear him say. Meshy fought on.

Addy grabbed Bucky by the shirt and dragged him toward Meshy. She couldn't just stand there and watch him get executed.

Before she got to Meshy and the men from across the road, the ground started to vibrate. Grains of desert sand danced on the ground like they were sitting on a giant drum head.

Addy watched as Number A's hand was suddenly tugged upward, over his head, the pistol raised to the air. The vibration intensified. Number A pulled at his raised hand with his free hand, trying to pry it from the sky that seemed to have it grasped firmly in its invisible clutch.

The pistol went off. A green laser beam shot from its muzzle. There were a series of white halos that emitted from the pistol, around the laser beam. It looked like something out of a Bugs Bunny cartoon.

The pistol was ripped from Number A's grip. It flung into the air in a great arc, its trajectory sending it up and over the top of Hamburger House.

The vibrations in the ground stopped immediately. Whatever held Number A's hand, let go.

"Meshy is gonna kill me for not recording this," Bucky said.

30

NUMBER A GAVE up the fight. He got up off Meshy's back.

"Ghost? That wasn't a ghost. That was Thwrp."

"Who the hell are you?" Paloma asked, sounding more like herself.

"Whoa, you're solid again." Bucky marveled.

Paloma had indeed become much less paranormal looking.

Meshy dusted himself off, "This place is even better than I could have imagined. It's not just the restaurant that's haunted, the whole damn property is haunted. Hell, I think we might even have some low-level demon possessions happening here. This is amazing!"

Addy thought Meshy had gone mad. She just got kidnapped. Basil was knocked out cold. Paloma became a ghost and Bucky was worried that he hadn't caught it on camera. Addy didn't need a camera to confirm what she knew they all just witnessed.

Number A shook his head. "Ghosts, you think we're dealing with ghosts out here?"

Paloma said, "I know we're dealing with ghosts out here." She stepped past Meshy and the man from across the road and attended to Basil.

Addy went to help her. She shot Meshy a dirty look as she moved past him.

"It's not ghosts," Number A said and glanced over at Number B who was still laid out in the road, but moving, "haven't you been reading the papers? We can barely contain the activity happening out here."

Basil came to, "UFOs," he rubbed the side of his head where he'd been pistol whipped and winced.

"UAPs, not UFOs," Number A said.

"No, EVP. Electronic voice phenomenon," Meshy said.

"Unexplained aerial phenomenon," Number A countered like he was Daffy Duck.

Meshy shot back with his best Bugs Bunny, "EVP!"

"UAP!"

"EVP!"

"UAP!"

"Alright, alright, stop!" Paloma cut in, "Look, I don't know about UFOs and UAPs and MTVs. I do know that I just experienced the most lucid full-body possession of my life. If you ask me what's going on, this place, this whole area, is possessed by demons. We are standing on the gates of Hell."

"Whoa!" Bucky wished he'd been recording Paloma for that. He could have added an ominous *DUN! DUN! DUN!* in post-production to really punch the moment. He thought it sounded pretty radical to add the demon angle to the story they'd been experiencing all day.

"Bucky! Damnit, go pick up the camera," Meshy demanded, always producing a television show, no matter what was going on around him.

Number A went to check on Number B. "Y'all need to stop filming. It'll never get to broadcast. The agency will see to that, you can be sure."

Paloma and Addy helped Basil to his feet. He was woozy but he could stand on his own.

"Would you mind telling us who you people are, anyway?" Addy asked.

"Can't tell you that," Number A said, slapping Number B across the face to get him revived.

"Maybe we need to call the police and have them tell us who you are," Addy threatened.

Meshy lowered his voice so the two men wouldn't hear him, "Addy, I think involving the authorities as this juncture may get our production shut down, if you catch my drift."

"Go on. Call 'em. See what good that does you," Number A said, dragging Number B to his feet.

"Look, I know as well as you do, who you guys are. So, what is it? Desert Ghost Hunters? Haunted Restaurants? Southwest Paranormal Activity? Huh? What's the name of the show you two are shooting?"

It was Number A's turn to lower his voice, "Wow, they think we're ghost hunters. Play along."

Then to Meshy he said, "Something like that anyway. You caught us."

"I knew that UAP nonsense was a distraction. Nobody in their right mind talks about that corny stuff. Listen, instead of kidnapping and assault, maybe we could work together?"

Number A couldn't believe they were that naive, "Ahh yeah. That would be great. Say, you guys got a psychic on your crew?"

"Sure do," Meshy said, pointing to Paloma.

"Oh, that's great. Yeah, we'd love to work with you."

"Awesome. Why don't you get your van off the road and we can get back to business inside? I'll have Basil get you up to speed."

Number A clapped Number B on the back, "Start the van. I'll grab the psychic and we'll get outta here, fast."

31

ADDY WALKED WITH BUCKY. They walked side by side. She leaned into his shoulder, staying close, seeking comfort. He was soft, like a fluffy, dumb blanket. She wanted to curl up around him and snuggle. She'd go anywhere with the goofball, even into a haunted house.

Meshy helped Basil along, back inside. Basil insisted he was fine but the lump on his head suggested otherwise. Basil was the pain in the ass of the team, but he was Meshy's pain in the ass and they *were* a team. Besides, Meshy laughed to himself, maybe the thunk on the head would get him to believe in ghosts.

Paloma followed behind Meshy and Basil. She kept playing the possession back in her mind. She couldn't process what had happened. Usually, when she channeled spirits, they spoke through her. She had control over everything. It was like being a translator, hearing someone speaking in one language and repeating it back in another. What happened to her on the side of Route 66 was different. It was almost as if she was trapped inside a deep dive suit looking through a porthole. She could see everything going on but the suit was controlling her movements. She could talk all she wanted, but nobody on the outside could hear her through the thick shell that she was encased by.

She didn't hate that feeling.

Number A caught up to Paloma, "Hey, so you're the psychic?"

Paloma gave Number A the side eye, "I don't trust you."

"Oh, come on. We're on the same team now. How are you able to communicate with them? Did they do the surgery on you when you were little?"

"I have no idea what you're talking about."

"Of course, you do. It's the only way. It's the gift, right? They told you that. That's what they tell all the psychics."

Paloma stopped. She flicked her hair over one side of her body with a jerk of the neck, "Or maybe, I was born with it, sweetheart."

"Feisty," Number A said, "I like that."

A voice spoke inside Paloma's mind, "*Steve.*"

"Why do they call you Number A, Steve?"

Number A's eyes opened as wide as saucers, "How could you know that?"

Paloma raised a smug eyebrow at him, "Psychic. Born with it."

She turned to keep walking. Meshy was holding the door opened, allowing Basil to hobble in. He paused for a moment and looked back at Paloma, then entered the building.

Number A grabbed Paloma's wrist, "We're not going in there."

Paloma yanked her arm back but Number A held tight, "Let go of me, *Steve.*"

He clamped harder around her arm at the mention of his real name, and pulled her toward the van. She saw the other guy, Number B, sitting in the driver's seat, one arm dangling out the window. He was snarling at her. Paloma wished she knew his name too.

"*Wendel.*"

"Wendel?" she asked aloud. That was the oddest name she'd ever heard in her life.

Number A paused again. He was annoyed with her for saying their real names aloud. That was totally against protocol. It threatened their safety. The agency didn't warn them about how dangerous this particular psychic could be. He would be leaving some very passive aggressive displeasure in his report when it was time to file.

Number B banged on the side of the van, "C'mon, let's go!"

"She knows your name," Number A said, still stunned.

"Number B?"

"No, Wendel."

Number B almost leaped out of the window, "You're not supposed to use my real name. Not ever. That's against protocol! I have to file a report now!"

"She said it, not me," Number A said, pissed at himself for uttering their civilian name also. He was going to need to file a report against himself too.

"Way to go, Steve," Number B said sarcastically.

That set off another round of 'Dudes' and 'You're not supposed to say my names' and 'I'm going to have to file a report on *you* nows' and 'Shit, I'm going to have to file a report on *me* now.'

For all their bickering, neither Number A, nor Number B noticed Paloma go translucent.

32

CRUMBLES WAS GETTING tired of this shit. He'd solved one problem but another arose. There were still two visitors to Hamburger House that were unruly, and they hadn't even gotten in the door yet.

They were trying to steal his customers again. Crumbles didn't like that at all.

The nervous woman had stepped into him. Maybe, this time, he could step into the tall woman? He ran as fast as his oversized clown shoes and one-piece clown romper would allow. He didn't need to attain Olympic speeds. The tall woman had said something and stopped her kidnapper dead in his tracks.

He charged into the tall woman's form as the man kidnapping the other woman began to argue with the other man driving the van. That's all the distraction he needed to catch up and move into the woman's space.

He hoped this would work!

Crumbles occupied the same space as the tall woman. Okay, now what? He didn't feel anything. He didn't feel like he was wearing her skin or looking through her eyes. He supposed they would both see the same things, standing in the same space, looking in the same direction.

He did a little clown dance, to see if maybe the woman would do the same clown dance. He wasn't sure how he would tell if the tall woman was doing the same dance if he was standing exactly where she was but he had to try something.

PALOMA BEGAN TO DANCE. SHE KICKED UP ONE KNEE IN FRONT OF her, brought it back down and then brought up her other knee. She wagged her arms at her side in time with the movements.

She lost control of herself again. She was occupied again. She didn't freak out. It was almost fun. She was reminded of that scene from Beetlejuice where the dinner guests are all forced to dance to a Harry Belafonte song. They weren't freaked out either, they thought it was as much fun as Paloma did.

As sudden as the dancing started it stopped.

Something else stopped too. Number A and Number B weren't arguing anymore. They were looking at Paloma like she'd grown a second head.

"SHE'S INVISIBLE!" NUMBER B SHOUTED FROM THE VAN.

"We can still see her, she's not invisible, you idiot." Number A stared, slack-jawed, at the psychic.

"You can see right through her. She's invisible."

"No, she's translucent, not invisible." Number A jabbed a finger at Paloma. The tip of his finger passed through her body. "Holy shit."

"Get her, and let's get outta here!" Number B called.

"I can't! It's like she's not there."

Number B got out of the van. It shouldn't be this hard to detain their target. He tried to grab hold of Paloma himself but his arms passed right through her. "Holy shit."

Number A stared at Number B with the 'I-told-you-so' look.

"Now what?"

. . .

CRUMBLES LAUGHED. IT WORKED! HE COULD HITCH A RIDE INSIDE THE bodies of the living! He reached out and honked one of the men's noses. The man flinched. He felt it! And yes, they couldn't lay a hand on Crumbles.

The celebration was tinged with one other realization. Something Crumbles suspected all along, but chose to ignore. He was dead. Dead a long, long time. He stood there, on the side of Route 66, watching the customers pass him by, not stopping anymore. He rationalized that the world had moved on, but it was Crumbles who'd moved on.

He'd died at some point. He thought he knew when it happened. Right about the same time he split from that angry Crumbles inside Hamburger House. It was his fault. He'd been the one who became impulsive. He was such an angry, angry clown. Crumbles understood why the angry version of himself acted the way he did. That Crumbles didn't like people stealing his customers either. That angry version of Crumbles did some things this Crumbles couldn't bear to bring to mind. It was awful what he did to that boy.

Crumbles left that behind. He decided to stay out on the roadside and beckon more customers inside. He'd remained there forever. But he was dead. That's why they didn't come anymore. He was a ghost. They couldn't see him. Nobody would ever stop for an old clown shilling for an empty shell of a roadside hamburger joint.

Maybe... Maybe they'd be able to see him now, the way these men could see him. Maybe he'd keep the body of the woman and stand on the side of the highway and welcome them all in again.

Yes! It will be glorious.

A GHOSTLY RED BALLOON SPROUTED FROM THE WOMAN'S HAND. A translucent red nose appeared on her nose. It was oversized, like her bug-eyed sunglasses. Paloma walked to the side of Route 66 and began to wave at cars only the clown could see.

Had any real cars full of real families been traveling past Hamburger House at that moment they would have been treated to a spectacle. They would have pulled into the parking lot of the deserted old burger joint for sure. Who wouldn't stop to look at a ghostly woman with a big red clown nose and bug-eyed designer sunglasses? And right behind her, two non-descript men hovering off the ground, swimming through the air. That was definitely a roadside attraction worth stopping for.

But, alas, the traffic along Route 66 was sparse. The cars all drove past at high speed along the new interstate only a couple of hundred yards away. The world missed out when it moved so fast.

33

THWRP CURSED. To human ears, his cursing would've sounded like a garbled mess of warbles and bleeps. To Thwrp, the curses were a delicately woven tapestry of F-bombs and S-words sprinkled with some choice versions of the 'B' and 'C' profanities.

The human he'd connected with was the one they kept trying to remove. If he was ever to get off this *bleep-garble-warble-whoop* rock, he was going to need that human to do it.

Thwrp was pretty sure the human was female. It was hard to tell, they were all so ugly. Humans gave him the heebie jeebies. They were creepy looking with their bulges, protrusions, and coarseness. Nothing at all like the sleek, streamline, form of his species. And the humans knew they were gross too, always covering up the nasty bits with fabrics to try and smooth their own forms.

Thwrp had no need for accouterments. He was hot as *warble-gloops-bleep-woo*. Like every other of his kind; every Thwrpian as perfect as the next. Why deviate from perfection? That was nature's way.

But nature had run amok on this planet they call Earf. Thwrp didn't want to be stuck among these grotesque beings. His craft was broken. He'd set down to make repairs but lacked an energy source strong enough to get his craft moving again.

Everything in the Thwrpian Galactic Guidebook indicated Earf was a planet of refuse. Yet, where he set down, not one smelly organic by-product rotted away. He required organic matter for fusion to power his thrusters. Curse the gravity of this planet. It held his ship down. Thwrp was affixed to its surface.

Thank goodness the human came along. He could touch her mind. Her neuro-receptors were wide open. Very rare for any Earfling, or the Sigh-Kick as he heard them all refer to her. The only issue was, everything that could communicate through her, did. His commlink to her brain was muddled. There were other neuro communicators attempting to utilize her as well.

Then these other humans step in and try to remove her. He couldn't let that happen. Thwrp could manipulate more than just minds.

When he thought he had a grip on the Sigh-Kick, she was overcome by another force. If he couldn't control the Sigh-Kick, he'd remove the other problem.

The two humans. They'd been present since he landed. Thwrp couldn't tell if they pinpointed his secret location or if they'd only detected him in the area. Either way, they'd been watching but not approaching.

The other group of humans, who'd arrived on this latest Earf day, disrupted their plans. Today was the first time the two humans had made a move. Thwrp was pretty sure they were local constables, very common on most worlds occupied by sentient beings. They shouldn't have been an issue for Thwrp. Earf was less advanced and wouldn't pose a threat. The Earflings understood cosmic populations existed, which was saying something but they were still a long way away from understanding the galactic community and where they stood in its echelons.

To immobilize these problem humans, Thwrp used the fabric of space and lifted them off the ground. Humans were only mobile on their hind quarters. Take that away and they are helpless to do anything. Still too stupid to understand how to use the fabric of space to their advantage. Too easy.

Thwrp decided he'd had enough of these Earflings and enough of Earf. He pulled the two humans to him through the fabric. Like reeling in Gwrp-Twrp from the red oceans back on Thwrpiter. Too *woop-beep-warble-oot-oot-burp* easy.

Now, if he could only get his hands on the Sigh-Kick. And some garbage.

34

MESHY WAS ready to get back to the production. They were close to wrapping this shoot. They'd already gathered incredible footage. All he had to do was capture a few one-shot confessionals and shoot a wrap up segment. Then they could spend the rest of the week in post-production.

There was light at the end of the tunnel in the dark New Mexican night.

There was also a bright light shining outside in the dark.

"What the hell?" Meshy cussed and walked to the window to see who was shining the bright light inside Hamburger House.

It wasn't a single source of light but two. Headlights. The two men must have been pulling their van off the road. As fellow ghost hunters they should have known better than to shine their head-lamps at the windows of the set. It would mess up the lighting for starters. Ghosts had a hell of a repulsion to bright lights. Plus, it made them harder to see.

He saw shadows dance against the headlights. Three figures, one in a skirt from the outline. Meshy could swear it almost looked like a struggle between the three. They stopped though and stood, the two in pants facing the skirt. Conversing perhaps?

And then the skirt, presumably Paloma, vanished. The dark silhouette she was casting disappeared, replaced by full on bright from the van's headlights.

"Bucky! Camera!" It was happening again and they were missing it. Meshy bolted out the door. That Bucky better damn sure come following on his heels like a good dog.

Meshy stepped outside. He angled himself away from the direct glow of the van's headlights. He could see Paloma. Sort of. She was there, but she was ghostly looking, an apparition. Oddly enough, she was holding a red balloon and wore an equally red clown nose.

Before he could call for Bucky again, the ground shook.

He heard a door open behind him. It had better be Bucky and he'd better have the camera rolling. Meshy dared not take his eyes off Paloma's ghost though. He didn't want to miss a moment of what he was seeing.

He heard Addy emerge behind him say, "Wow."

"Yeah. Wow. Bucky, are you getting this?"

"Rolling," came Bucky's voice as the ground began to rumble beneath their feet.

"Earthquake." Basil said.

"The ghosts." Meshy said.

The two men with Paloma rose off the ground several feet. Meshy had never seen anything like it in his life, except for maybe a magic show. But magic was an illusion and ghosts were real. They were witnessing actual paranormal spiritual manipulation. The ghosts were physically manipulating human beings!

Everyone was going to be talking about Not Normal Investigations TV!

The two men swam in the air, arms and legs waving about, trying to get themselves back to the ground. The ghosts wouldn't let up. Meshy noticed Paloma, dancing like a clown, oblivious to the two men swimming above her.

Was she possessed by the same spirits manipulating the men? Maybe Paloma was somehow levitating them. Had she tapped into deeper psychic powers she never before discovered? All Meshy knew was they were going to be rich!

"Bucky! Camera on me, now!"

Bucky panned the camera from the two floating men onto Meshy and Basil.

"We're capturing never-seen-before footage of actual human/spirit physical interaction. There is no manipulation on our part. Seeing is believing. Basil, what possible explanation do you have for what we are witnessing right now?"

Basil wasn't ready to be put on the spot. He was still trying to process what was transpiring. There had to be a logical conclusion. He just didn't have it. The data was coming in too quickly. The last thing he wanted to do was admit that there may be some sort of paranormal activity taking place. That was never the case. Ultimately, there was always a logical explanation.

"There's always a logical explanation. I'll need some time to process what we are witnessing. It is pretty incredible, though."

Bucky panned back on the two men floating above the ground. They began to float slowly along the ground, toward Hamburger House.

Meshy was relishing his moment of triumph over Basil, "Ha! I got you to admit it! I got the skeptic to admit we are filming actual ghosts!"

"That's not what I said."

"Uhm, guys," Bucky interrupted as he watched the two men float off around the side of Hamburger House. "They're getting away."

"Shit! Follow them!" Meshy said, taking chase.

Basil and Bucky followed. The shaky camera work added a nice touch of drama to the scene.

Paloma, inhabited by the ghost of Crumbles, continued to dance along the side of Route 66, happily waiting for more potential customers to pass.

35

TYPICAL MEN. They left Paloma dancing by herself in the desert. Addison wasn't about to leave her there alone.

Addy could see right through Paloma as if she were made of rice paper. She thought about the experience she'd had at the side of Route 66. Seeing a place and time that was long ago and long gone. She wondered if that was how she appeared as well?

All this time Addison had been frightened of ghosts she never believed in. To see Paloma in the state she was, translucent and not herself at all, put the ghosts into perspective. How could something acting with pure joy be something she thought was malicious? She had a face to put on her ghosts now and she could even put her own face to the phenomenon.

Maybe this place was haunted. Maybe that wasn't so bad.

"Paloma?" Addy asked as if she was interrupting something important.

Paloma continued to dance but stopped and glanced at Addy, "Say! I know you! Come on in and have a burger and fries! Don't forget to wash it down with an ice-cold pop!"

Addy took a step back. That was not Paloma's sultry, exotic voice at all. The voice that came out of her mouth was dopey and masculine, almost like that goofy cartoon dog. The voice of Crumbles the Clown. He possessed Paloma.

"I... I will," Addy stammered, apprehensive about addressing Paloma as Crumbles the Clown, "I'd like to enjoy a meal with my friend though. Can I borrow her back?"

Crumbles knew what he was doing. He knew he was inside Paloma. It was obvious he would have to give her up to allow his customers to enjoy a meal. That was the whole point after all. Crumbles was both happy and sad despite the emotion painted on his face.

He nodded to Addy and winked. He offered the ghostly red balloon that Paloma was holding to Addison. Addy reached out and took it, she felt like a little girl. Balloons were happy things. Addy pinched the translucent string between her fingers and Crumbles let go. The balloon popped and Paloma was once again opaque.

"Paloma?" Addy put a hand out to steady the woozy woman.

Paloma cast the back of her wrist across her forehead. A classic dramatic posture for a classically, dramatic woman. She wouldn't faint. Paloma was too strong for that garbage. Instead, she took a deep breath and stood tall.

Addy looked at Paloma not knowing what to say. Saying something like, 'Well, that was fucked up.' was a bit too on the nose for the moment. She deferred to Paloma to address the moment.

"Well, that was fucked up." Paloma said.

Addy giggled, "I was gonna say..."

"Was I like you?" Paloma asked, "You know, like... see-through?"

Addy nodded.

"You couldn't see my boobies or anything, right? Not like that kind of see through?"

"No. Just kinda like you were fog, I guess. Clothed but foggy."

They both laughed. What else was there to do?

"Where are the others?" Paloma asked, realizing it was just the two of them in the desert evening.

"Oh! Those two weird guys floated off behind the building. The boys chased after them."

Paloma didn't remember anything about floating men. She only recalled them trying to coax her into their van. They were becoming forceful about it but then she didn't remember much. She knew she was dancing and happy. But other details were hazy.

"You were somewhere else, weren't you?"

Paloma told Addy about old cars passing by. She told her about the faces of happy children. It felt good when children laughed and smiled at you. It was the kind of glee that made you want to dance.

Addison knew exactly what Paloma was talking about. She stepped into Crumble's world as well. That clown was so jovial being here, at Hamburger House. This was his happy place and he was never going to leave it.

Maybe, this was his Heaven.

36

THE TWO MEN from across the road hovered behind Hamburger House in front of a green dumpster. The dumpster looked new, covered in a fresh, green glossy coat of paint and a smooth black lid that looked like it was ceramic more than plastic.

The lid lifted open. The motion was smooth, as if driven by a piston and not some derelict that was living inside. The lid stopped with a hiss after opening its maw about a foot high. The bum living inside the dumpster poked his head up.

His head was oddly shaped. It was oversized and irregular, like something a child formed with a ball of clay. The bum's neck was thin, too thin to hold up such a bulbous meatloaf of a head. Yet, it did. The face was gray with a brownish pallor and not a hair on its head.

Bleep-garble-weep-boop-boop.

If the two men across the road knew how to speak Thwrpian, they would have known Thwrp had said, "Look at these two shit stains they sent to find me."

The Earflings hadn't even received intergalactic language translation training. Rookies, they sent rookies out for Thwrp. How the heck was he expected to get his ship re-powered when they sent him out quick-lube mechanics?

Without power to his craft, Thwrp couldn't be positive that Earf was even a member of the Intergalactic League of Inter-Galaxies and Collectibles. But it had to be. Why else would there be a tier one rescue and recovery team on site? They were the roadside assistance of the galaxy. Every ILIG&C planet had them. Granted these two bumpkins were only capable of jumping power cores, fixing flat tires and towing any craft that required further assistance back to the garage.

Thwrp wasn't even sure they could accomplish that much. Just look at their service module, or what they described as a 'van'. It might be able to get Thwrp's scout craft in for service, but there was no way that thing would be capable of towing a run-of-the-mill class III star cruiser from the ionosphere to the stratosphere. Ridiculous.

Worse yet, Thwrp couldn't even talk to these two bozos. No language training whatsoever and their minds were dead as door-nails so psychic transmission was useless as well. He needed a trans-lator. He reached out for the other Earfling. The one he tapped into earlier who wasn't part of the ILIG&C crew.

"Hang on a minute. Let me get someone who can actually help me out here." knowing full well all the two humans heard was *Thwr-rbl-Wrrbl-Nurp-Glurp-Blrrrr.*

As Thwrp reached out to the other human's mind he made a mental note to also ask to see their ILIG&C curio cabinet. He'd have to grab an Earf collectible or two for the journey back. His loin nuggets always enjoy gifts from exotic planets. Though Thwrp was hesitant to consider Earf exotic given the level of service and hospi-tality he'd received so far.

There was a time when you could land anywhere in the tri-galaxy area and have your portholes cleaned and your lubricants checked for proper viscosity. Those days were fading. They were already gone on Earf.

Thwrp had trouble tapping into the other human. Her mind was preoccupied. Were there other intergalactic travelers around using her services, he wondered? For such a barren landscape, this Earf sure seemed rather busy.

He reached out again.

37

MESHY HELD up at the back corner of the building. He didn't want to round the bend and get ambushed by the two men. Basil and Bucky halted behind him, hugging the building close. Bucky kept the camera trained on Meshy.

Meshy peeked around the corner. When he did, he dropped to one knee but kept looking around the bend.

"What's going on?" Bucky asked.

Meshy waved his hand at Bucky to be quiet.

Basil leaned over Meshy and peered around the back of the building. He, too, kept looking at something happening behind the Hamburger House.

"Basil, what's going on?" The mystery drove Bucky crazy. He was the one with the camera. Shouldn't he see what was going on too? He was supposed to capture everything.

Basil waved his hand at Bucky. There was no way for Bucky to shoot around the corner. He couldn't reach over Basil or crouch lower than Meshy. He'd have to come away from the side of the building and stand in the open.

Fuck it. If he listened to Meshy and stayed back, he would just catch shit for not filming whatever it was they were seeing. And, if he did jump out from the side of the building to do what he knew in his heart Meshy would want, he'd get shit for that too. He stepped around Meshy and Basil, using the viewfinder as his eyes.

The camera captured the scene of the two floating men they'd chased hovering in front of an odd, green dumpster. At first, it looked like there was a glob of old meat piled up inside high enough to keep one of the lid's propped open. Bucky zoomed in and saw the pile of old meat had eyes and those eyes widened when they honed in on Bucky and the camera.

Bucky was frozen. What the fuck was that thing? His finger depressed the zoom button on the camera. He wasn't supposed to narrate from behind the camera. Another one of Meshy's production rules. He couldn't help himself though, "That's one fucked up looking ghost," he said, breaking another production rule. No swearing.

Meshy went into director/talent mode. He jumped in front of the camera. He wasn't sure what to make of the scene just yet. Bucky was right, that was one fucked looking ghost. He half-cursed, half-thanked Bucky for his brazen act. No turning back now.

"We're in the back of Hamburger House witnessing something extraordinary. Actual, tangible, paranormal activity. In short, not only do we have a ghost but it is a *physical* ghost. There's no other way to explain it folks. I'm as stupefied as you."

Blurdle-blurdle-blurdle-glrrr-nurpburp-nurp-burp

Meshy turned his back to the camera, stunned by the vocalization from the ghost.

From the corner of the building, out of the shot, Basil said, "That's not a ghost Meshy. That's an extraterrestrial being!"

Bucky swung the camera to Basil. Basil grimaced and grabbed Bucky by the shoulder, dragging him out of the line of sight.

"Basil! What did you do that for, man?" Bucky said, "Quit fucking around."

Bucky took a step to get back into position. Basil held him where he was. "Look."

Meshy was airborne.

Bucky raised the camera back up, capturing Meshy flailing in the air as he levitated a few feet off the ground.

38

PALOMA COVERED HER EARS.

"Paloma, what's wrong? Is it the ghost again?"

Paloma couldn't answer. Her mind was being assaulted. She didn't think it was Crumbles. Her body wasn't being inhabited. This was something pushing into her mind again. She was a psychic, used to channeling the thoughts of spirit energies. Whatever was tapping into her mind now was powerful and forceful. Her ears squealed and this energy bore into her brain waves. She couldn't battle it. The force felt as if it would split her skull in half.

Paloma felt Addy comforting her. Addy begged her to tell her what was happening. She couldn't talk. She could only wince away from the pain.

And then it stopped and her mind felt... open. She could hear things from everywhere. She had tapped into another dimension. The sensation was incredible. And in this plane, a voice spoke to her, "Get these two jerks to gas up my ride. It's time for me to jet, sister."

Paloma looked at Addy, "Did you just say that?"

Addy frowned, "Say what? I asked if the ghost was inside of you again? Are you okay?"

"I've been made. Gotta blast. Get back here. Help me out, sister."

"There it is again!" Paloma said. She was looking right at Addy. Her lips didn't move but she heard the voice like it came from in front of her. Just like earlier, inside Hamburger House, during the cash register segment. "We need to go around back. I've gotta help my brother out."

"Your brother?" Addy asked. She thought maybe Paloma had gone insane. All the possessions had broken her mind. "Okay, let's get you back where the others are. They can help you." She led Paloma in the direction the boys had run off around the back of the building.

This place was a circus. Why was she so adamant about selling it? She didn't think she could do it any longer. How could she allow somebody to go through what she and the Not Normal Production team had gone through today? If something happened to somebody, she'd never be able to forgive herself.

Maybe Hamburger House was Addison's cross to bear? It could be the universe had put the burden of this place on her because she was the only one capable of handling its weight. She didn't have to live here or anything. She just had to keep everyone away.

Never sell. Just let it be abandoned in the middle of nowhere. Let the spirits be here alone. Nobody could get hurt, on either plane of existence.

As the two women rounded the corner the men had taken, Addison stated, "I think I'm going to take down the 'For Sale' signs."

Then she saw past Bucky and Basil. She saw Meshy hovering in mid-air. She thought maybe she spoke too soon.

39

THWRP TAPPED INTO THE WOMAN. She had a powerful connection.
She would have been happy living among the Thwrpians. Thwrpians were natural psychic beings. Few humans had developed
psychic ability. Primitive.

"Come closer, sister." He beckoned to the woman who was just
around the side of the building where the others were hiding.

She was being held back. That's what she told Thwrp. She didn't
seem distressed. Her compatriots were looking out for her safety.
They thought he was a threat. They kept referring to him as a ghost.
Thwrp didn't know what a ghost was. Probably another
intergalactic race he was not familiar with. The ghosts must be
hostile, because the humans were cautious about exposing themselves to these ghost beings.

Thwrp could touch the minds of the humans. He found no
connection with the ghosts. They were a neuro-blocking race if that
was the case. Very dangerous. Neuro blocking beings were always
trouble in the galaxy. They were always up to no good since their
minds, and thus their motives, could not be read. Criminals,
through and through.

It mattered not. The task at hand was tapping into the energy

Thwrp was reading inside of the building. There was lots of it. Enough to power up his craft and get him off this rock full of lesser beings.

Thwrp pulled the other human he'd manipulated in line with the other two. He reached out to the woman and told her they'd all be safe if she helped him. He was sure to call her sister. It was a term he'd picked up scanning the human broadcast signals, in search of the ILIG&C emergency channels. They'd say things like, 'You're my sister, and I love you' or 'Let's go sing songs of rejoice, sister.' or 'We're not supposed to do things like that, I'm your sister.' It was a word that signaled deep companionship among the humans. Thwrp used it to his advantage.

"Tell them it's okay. I will not manipulate any more of them as long as you can get me access to the energies within the building. I am your sister. And you are mine. We are all sisters of the universe."

Thwrp could be poetic when he wanted. Had he not chosen to become a Thwrpian Intergalactic Scout, he would have pursued the thespian arts (or, in Thwrpian language, what was roughly translated to as 'fancy-ass cosplay'). It was a noble art that appealed to the Thwrpmanity in all. His mother would never have approved.

The human communicated his intentions to the others. There was debate. Trust was an issue. More talk of the ghosts. These ghosts were putting a wrench in an otherwise simple operation.

"I'm not of the ghostly persuasion. I'm Thwrpian, of the planet Thwrp. My name is Thwrp, like my father before me. And his father. And his father's father. And my friend's father. Also, my mother's father's name was Thwrp as well. It is a good name. A Thwrpian name. A name you can trust. Thwrp."

The woman communicated his assurances.

The tone of their negotiation changed. Things were looking up. The energy within the building amplified. He could feel it.

40

BUCKY AND BASIL WERE CONFUSED. Something had changed. Whatever was communicating with Paloma was not acting like a ghost. What was it? Paloma had talked a lot about Thwrps. It was an odd word neither of them understood.

"Could be ancient Sumerian," Bucky suggested. He had no formal education on ancient cultures and their dialects. He thought maybe he heard it in Ghostbusters.

"Bucky. You know I don't believe in things like ghosts, right?" Basil asked.

Bucky nodded.

"Well, just because I'm skeptical about paranormal activity doesn't mean I don't believe in any weird phenomenon."

Bucky nodded.

"Like, extra-terrestrials?"

Bucky nodded.

"Bucky, I'm suggesting this Thwrp thing communicating with Paloma isn't a meat shaped spirit blob hiding in a dumpster. I'm suggesting it may be a meat shaped alien hiding in a dumpster."

Bucky nodded, "Cool."

"So maybe, we take a leap of faith and help it."

Bucky nodded.

Basil supposed what he really wanted was for Bucky to play the skeptic for once. He wished Bucky would pause for a moment and consider reason. He wanted Bucky to tell him he was being crazy. Aliens weren't real. But Bucky romanticized the idea of supernatural things like ghosts and aliens. He wanted them to be real, because, without them, the world was boring.

Basil, using his own sense of logic and reason, had always left open the possibility that alien civilization existed. The universe was far too vast not to contain a cornucopia of life, grander than Basil could fathom. He could question aliens having ever visited Earth, there was reason to be skeptical about that. But to think that Earth was the only planet in the known and unknown universe was mad.

But now, there was evidence in a meat shaped figure hiding in a dumpster behind the Hamburger House. The house they'd spent all day looking for ghosts could very well be haunted. Not by spirits but by aliens.

It all made sense. All the research he'd been doing today on Bard and San Jon kept bringing up articles about UFO sightings. Those were easy to discredit, especially when you lived in New Mexico. But now, faced with an alien looking creature, three hovering bodies and psychic contact with Paloma, it was impossible for his skeptic mind to deny.

"Aliens." Basil affirmed.

He let go of Paloma who stepped into the open. Basil stood out in the open next to her. Bucky kept filming. Addy hugged close to Bucky, putting her head against his back, taking comfort in his warmth.

Basil and Paloma began to float. They didn't flail like the others. They knew what was coming and they knew not to fight it. There was elation on their faces, like they'd seen God. And he was good.

41

THANK YOU, *sister.*

I require the energy amassed within this building for my craft. Have your kind access this energy so that I may bind it to my vessel. Once the craft has sufficient fuel, I will take my leave of Earf. Reports will be filed with the ILIG&C. However, I will note in the comments section about your particular cooperative efforts. The personal fines imposed on you will be far less severe than the others.

Oh, and if you could also secure a trinket from the gift shop, that would be swell. Nothing too big, but something nice. Something memorable and Earfy. I was thinking one of those cat-soup packets would be wonderful. Those seem to be exemplary relics of Earf. Perhaps bring me two of those. And a single-wrapped plastic straw for my wife. The kind that winds up in the ocean, stuck in sea creatures' noses. When I think of Earf, I think of sea creatures with plastic straws in their olfactory canals. Very collectible.

Also, could you not mention my presence to these ghost creatures everyone keeps mentioning. I'm not familiar with their kind and I'd prefer to avoid any... diplomatic incursions, if at all possible.

Don't forget the energy, sister. That's most important.

Oops! Almost forgot. Here, take this. As payment. Let it be known that Thwrp is not a freeloader. I insist on paying for my collectibles. It's a

Thwrpian Blowtorch. If you need to produce combustion, all you do it press the red button. The one marked 'THWRP' That will engage the catalyst reaction to engage the thermal energy release. But you knew that already. What else would a button marked 'THWRP' do?

I can see from your memory banks, you describe this payment as a lighter. Very popular in your gift shops. You can sell it as a trinket to the visiting Earflings. A fair trade and a wonderful opportunity to market the great planet of Thwpiter as a place to consider for your next travel destination. The Thwrpian Chamber of Commerce will be very pleased. Very pleased indeed.

I really appreciate this. I'd do it all myself but gravity is a bitch. I mean, look at me. My body wasn't built for this type of G-Force. I look like a Thwrploaf on a stick. It's embarrassing.

You know what? If everything goes okay, pick out something nice for yourself as well. I'll charge it to my ILIG&C account. Nothing for your friends though. They were kinda dickish. Especially these two. Total creepers.

Off you go. I'll keep your friends here, safe and sound until you get back.

42

MESHY HAD LOST CONTROL, in every way possible. The dumpster ghost had suspended him in midair. It had also gained psychic control over Paloma, it seemed. He wished he'd had his GeoPort, the ghost was uttering a series of warbles, bleeps, bloops, blops and grumbles. He guessed it was communicating with Paloma, because after a time the dumpster ghost shut up and Paloma walked away as if she'd been instructed to do something.

Meshy decided to go into investigator mode, "We're not here to hurt you. Please let me go and you can tell me your story. I have cameras, I can share your story with the world."

The dumpster ghost warbled, mumbled, tittered, and bleeped.

"I can hear you but I can't understand you. I have tools that can help me listen to you better. Will you let me go get them?

Mmmrble-nrble-brreeble-blrkk

"I'm not going to run away. I promise. You are the most spectacular thing I've ever witnessed. If you'll just let me down, I can help you. I have friends, we all can help you."

Breep.

Meshy had no way of knowing if he was appealing to the dumpster ghost's sensibilities. It was frustrating. At least when he was communicating with energies he couldn't see, he had a better sense of getting through to them and knowing if his efforts were falling on deaf ears.

And if he wasn't getting anywhere, he always had an ace up his sleeve. Or, in his pocket to be more precise. The fact of the matter was, ghosts were not as easy to find as Meshy would have hoped when he started Not Normal Investigations.

He believed in ghosts, one hundred percent. He haunted paranormal shops more often than the ghosts themselves. He interacted with mediums, psychics, astrophysicists and investigators and learned all there was to learn. He started out in cemeteries like most amateurs. His first investigative tool, an old 35mm Kodak camera his grandfather gave him a long time ago.

He found the usual, orbs and mists. A few photos he snapped showed something that could be considered an apparition if you wanted to believe so. Some might think the figures looked like bugs, overexposed from being too close to the lens when the flash went off. Those were the skeptics, always ready to shoot down any tiny suggestion that there were other things beyond our reality. Meshy despised the skeptics. They shit on his parade for his entire professional life.

He was never deterred by them. In fact, the naysayers only drove him to investigate more, to find definitive proof that not a single person on Earth could say was anything other than a ghost. And now, his whole future depended on breaking the will of a skeptic. Two in fact.

Meshy met a man named Bartholomew Bartleby. He insisted Meshy call him Bart. Bart had money. Bart was a skeptic. Bart also loved watching ghost hunter shows on TV. The only problem was, Bart believed they were all bullshit. Bart had seen a few videos of Meshy's investigations on YouTube and thought that Meshy's style had promise.

So, they met one afternoon at a coffee shop outside of Albuquerque. Bart agreed to produce the show. Meshy had full control. Only one caveat: Meshy had to have a skeptic on the team. No other ghost shows used a skeptic. Bart argued a skeptic would work to validate Meshy's investigations. If the skeptic had no qualms with Meshy's findings then, boom, ghosts must be real.

Fucking skeptics. He fought with them his whole life and now a skeptic was his ticket to the good life.

"How's this for proof, Basil, you son of a bitch!?"

Meshy bet Basil was still hiding, like a coward. Skeptics always shit their pants when things get real.

"Bucky! You incompetent poop, you better be filming this ghost. This is gold!" he called out to Bucky, who was probably still hiding like a little bitch with Basil.

Meshy stuck his tongue out at the meat ghost.

"That's an alien, Meshy!" he heard Bucky yell from his hiding spot.

Meshy regarded the meat ghost again. It was rather *real* looking for a ghost.

Meep.

43

Paloma walked past Bucky, Basil and Addy. She didn't regard them, instead, continued past to the front of Hamburger House.

Addy and Basil ran after her.

"Wait. Paloma! Where are you going?" Addy called after her.

Basil beckoned Bucky, "Come on!"

"No way," Bucky said, "I think I need to help Meshy."

"What are you going to do? That thing is going to grab you and hold you off the ground like the others."

"Yeah, but Meshy will kill me if I don't help."

Basil sighed, "Suit yourself." He chased after Paloma and Addy.

Paloma rounded the corner and went for the front door.

Addy placed her hand over Paloma's as she grabbed the door handle. "What are you doing?"

Paloma looked at Addy. All Addy could see were her dark, bug-eyed sunglass lenses, "I need to tap into the energy."

"Energy? What are you talking about? Is this Paloma? Am I talking to Paloma right now?"

Addy wondered if the ghost was back inside the statuesque woman or if maybe that thing out back was in charge now.

Hamburger House was officially a three-ring circus instead of a haunted house.

Basil came up behind the two women. "Paloma? Are you okay?"

Paloma yanked at the door handle. Addy prevented her from pulling it open.

"She's possessed again. I think."

"It's the alien. It's tapped into her. It's been tapped into her all day."

Addy twisted her neck and looked at Basil, "Tapped in? Like psychic powers? Is the skeptic suggesting psychic powers are real?"

"I'm suggesting a lot of crazy things all of a sudden."

"Is this because of all the UFO stuff you've been reading about while researching today?"

Basil shrugged, "We *are* in New Mexico."

"Alien capital of the world." Addy finished.

"You saw it. That thing in the dumpster isn't a ghost. That thing is sentient. Alive. Ghosts don't manipulate physical objects like that."

"Wow, sure sounds to me like you just gave credence to the existence of ghosts Basil."

"It's been a weird day."

Just like Bugs Bunny would have, Paloma slipped inside Hamburger House while Addy and Basil waxed intellectually the reality of all manner of paranormal creatures.

Simultaneously, they looked at each other and commented, "Shit," as they realized Paloma had snuck in while they were distracted by the conjecture.

When Addy and Basil got inside, they saw Paloma standing in the lobby, her arms spread out to her sides and her head tilted back toward the ceiling. Every piece of electronic equipment was buzzing, beeping and binging.

Paloma too, was buzzing, beeping, and binging. She was also warbling, grumbling, and whooping. A faint, blue, beam was streaming, like a cloud, from all the equipment to the center of Paloma's chest.

She was fueling up.

44

ANGRY CRUMBLES WAS ANGRY. They were stealing from his restaurant again. He knew the nervous woman wanted to steal from him all along. Every time he chased her away, she returned with more people. They could not have what was his. He swore he would never ever let anyone take what was his ever again. He was angry all the time. He didn't feel like himself. The only way he was ever going to find peace again was to protect what was his.

He wanted to be left alone. The Hamburger House was all he had left. Why did everyone want to take it away from him? The thought enraged him more and more!

This time the nervous woman returned with an army. They were not scared of him. They badgered him. Nothing detoured them. The more he tried to scare them away the more curious they became about his tactics. And they had power.

He'd never experienced anyone like the pretty woman with the group. She was like a beacon. An open microphone. He was drawn to her like a moth to a flame. She felt him. She could hear him. She was amazing.

And now, she was taking everything he had left.

Crumbles felt helpless as she sapped the energy out of

Hamburger House. He felt helpless as he watched his only friend, Ko, taken from him too.

Enough was enough. He couldn't battle back. There was little energy left to harness. He was powerless to stop it.

The dust! He drew in the dust.

GET OUT!

STOP!

MINE!

The woman was in a trance, stealing the essence of Hamburger House.

Two others came into the restaurant. One was the nervous woman who first came. The woman who brought the thieves. He grew furious. Crumbles stopped writing in the dust. He used every ounce of his anger and focused not on manipulating tiny particles of dust but the whole sheet of dust covering the counter.

POOF!

The dust exploded off the counter in a plume.

The woman shrieked. The man who came in with her hugged the pretty woman robbing Hamburger House. He stepped in the way of the energy beam. The exchange slowed to a trickle.

"Shut it down Ko! Shut it down!"

Ko was a good employee. He turned the fryolator on and off when he was told. He was winded but dragged himself to his station and shut down the machine.

The lights went out again.

Hamburger House began to charge up, fueled by Crumbles' anger. He instructed Ko to keep the fryolator off. Ko assured Crumbles he would not turn it on. Crumbles told Ko it would take time to build their strength back up. Then, they could chase the intruders away once more.

They would have to do something bigger than they'd done before. This was a new kind of enemy. Crumbles would need more power. He needed Crumbles, his good half. His happy half. He needed to become one again.

How was he going to convince Good Crumbles it was time to

come inside? A paradox. He needed to be whole again. He hoped Happy Crumbles understood that.

If not, the thing they were both happy and angry about would be lost forever.

45

THWRP CHECKED the systems on his craft. The Earfling was conducting the energy. He could practically taste it. His craft was ready to go. He'd be off this rock in no time. Speeding back to Thwrp and the other Thwrpians. Home in time for a fine meal of roast Thwrp and steamed Thwrp. All prepared lovingly by his wife, Thwrp.

He longed for home. Earf was interesting, in a primitive way. Perhaps he'd pack up the family sometime and bring them here for a little get away. But not until he squared away all his diplomatic complaints with the ILIG&C. These Earflings still had a lot to learn about peace and goodwill to their fellow intergalactarians.

Earf would never survive the wrath of Thwrpian sanctions. Their warships were very powerful. The type of ships that applied economic pressure by evaporating oppressive worlds to mist. Very persuasive.

Diplomacy was preferred over sanctions.

Besides, it would be a shame to vaporize all the Earfly collectibles. They had some nice trinkets around here.

Thwrp's mind jerked. His eye twitched. The Earflings he held in suspense dropped, their rumps bumped the ground before he regained control of them. The energy transfer had become inter-rupted. He searched the mind of the Earfling he'd tapped into. There was an... abruption.

Communication with the Earfling was muddled. There were cross-energies confusing the mind. Something was amiss. If he couldn't get the fuel, he'd be stuck on this rock another sol cycle and that was one cycle too long.

He needed to get inside and see with his own ocularies what the problem was. Thwrp's biggest problem, one he didn't wish to announce lest he give up his only weakness to the natives, was that Earf's gravity was too severe for his body. It weighed heavily on his physical anatomy. It made him appear frumpy like a pile of melted, rotting Thwrp.

Through his mind he could lift other objects against the great gravity of the planet, yet he was immobilized within his craft.

If only he could communicate with one of the three beings in front of him. He could use them as his vessel and ride them inside the building.

Mrrp-blrrp-grrble-blrrrp

The three stared at him, dumbfounded. He could try a psychic connection with the nimble minded again but he'd have to break the connection with the being he already grasped. It may be foolish but his connection with the other Earfling was muddled as it was.

Desperate times called for desperate measures. He broke the connection and reached out to the being wearing the soft helmet. The headwear seemed a foolish piece of apparatus, it would never cushion a cranial blow. It was full of tiny holes, fabricated of some type of cloth and had a silly duck bill on the front that would only save him from an attack of solar rays. It was foolish looking safety equipment. The gear wouldn't even protect his cranium against the force of air. Perhaps then, it served as some sort of cranial antenna.

Thwrp wagered his psychic connection on the one with the soft helmet antenna. He focused mind to mind.

Thwrp felt something. Was he in? A connection? Maybe, perhaps the cerebrum was so primitive it was like tapping into a thoughtless creature. That didn't seem right. How could the mind of one Earfling differ so vastly from another? Intelligence was relative.

"Hello?" Thwrp heard inside his own mind.

"Hello?" Thwrp questioned back.

"Whoa. Are you the ghost?" the voice in Thwrp's mind answered back.

"I am not of the ghost species. I am Thwrp of the Thwrpians from planet Thwrp."

In front of him, the Earfling laughed aloud.

"This is not funny. There is a serious problem. You will take me to the other Eaflings inside."

"Earflings? Geez you even talk like an alien. Are you a dead alien? How are you in my mind?"

"Quiet Earfling! You are my vessel. I am your pilot. You will take me to the energy source. Now!"

Thwrp was frustrated. He'd established a connection with the feeble mind but he held no sway. How could something so weak resist his compulsion? The stronger mind had no problem bending to his will. Was this thing so stupid it didn't know how to carry out commands?

"Hey! I'm not stupid. You idiot!" the Earfling argued, hearing Thwrp's own thoughts. This was a completely open connection. Amazing.

Thwrp played along, "You are stupid. You're not even smart enough to pick me up and carry me inside the building to your friends."

"Oh yeah! Put me down and I'll show you I ain't so stupid, I can do that!"

Thwrp set down the soft-helmeted human. He held the other two in his grasp.

The Earfling approached and flung the hatch of Thwrp's vessel open. He reached in and plucked Thwrp from within. Earf's massive gravity tugged at him hard around the waist. It was extremely painful.

"You are smart enough to know that I must ride upon your anterior, aren't you?" Thwrp asked soft-helmet.

"Anterior? Oh, my back? Yeah! Of course, I know that. I just need to adjust my grip and," the soft-helmeted being manipulated Thwrp over his head and placed him on his anterior side, "There we go."

Thwrp flung his lanky arms around the Earfling's cranial stem. The remainder of his weight distributed evenly across the Earflings wide anterior. It was rather comfortable.

"Okay. Take me to the energy Earfling!"

The soft-helmet moved forward with Thwrp on his back. The other two Earflngs floated along behind the caravan.

Thwrp wouldn't be held back from his energy any longer. Now that he was mobile, he was unstoppable. He'd wager a nifty collectible that these so-called ghost beings were behind this mayhem. A new enemy of the galaxy. Thwrp would be the first to face them.

What glorious stories he would have to share with Thwrp and the other Thwrpians back home!

46

If Angry Crumbles couldn't get Happy Crumbles to come inside, he would have to go outside to fetch him. Why not? He'd watched his jovial half inhabit the body of the nervous woman and now it was his turn.

He merged with the woman. He felt like he'd passed through a bubble. The sensation was odd, like he was wearing another clown suit over his own, but it had no weight. He raised his hand in front of his face and saw the smaller hand of a woman. He looked down. Breasts, not pom-poms, on his jumpsuit.

He moved to the picture frame. The portrait of himself. He saw the face of the young woman reflected in the glass, superimposed over the painting of his own visage. He touched his hand to the side of his face. The woman did the same. He was her.

He could leave!

He could incorporate into his happy half and be whole again.

He would be one and in control of Hamburger House again.

Crumbles led the woman's body to the door. She ran funny because he ran funny. Crumbles still wore clown shoes. They weren't that different from heels in the grand scheme of things.

Crumbles pushed open the door and rammed into a man wearing a hat with an alien draped on his back.

47

NOW WHAT? Addy was normal one moment and the next she was acting like she discovered she existed. She examined her hand, ran to the clown's portrait and looked at herself in the mirror. She looked curious about her own features.

Her eyes widened and she bolted for the door. She ran funny, like she was wearing clown shoes. A woman high stepping in heels looked ridiculous.

Addy opened the door. Meshy was there to greet her. The meat alien was on his back.

"Move," Addy demanded.

"No, get back inside. I need to deal with the ghost," Meshy told Addy.

"I *am* the ghost! And *you* can't have my house." Addy protested.

"I don't want the house. I want the energy."

"I'm the energy!" Addy pointed back inside at the fryolator, "He's the energy. We are the Hamburger House."

Meshy pushed Addy back inside. The two men from the desert floated in behind him.

Basil understood. The alien took control of Meshy's mind. The ghost of Crumbles the Clown possessed Addy's body

Basil elbowed Bucky, "You better be filming this."

"Jeez," Bucky muttered, "you too? I'm getting it, I'm getting it."

"Turn the energy back on!" Meshy demanded as he corralled Addy toward the fryolator.

"You can't have my energy! You'll kill me and Ko! Let me be whole again and there will be enough energy for everyone."

Basil eyed Paloma in his peripherals. She was standing as stiff as a statue. She seemed to glow with a blue aura. Semi-charged with the alien's blue energy, stolen from the ghosts of Hamburger House.

Addy said they were the energy. Was the alien killing the ghosts? Meshy often used the term 'energy' during his investigations. Did he understand something about the nature of ghosts?

Basil cursed himself, he was thinking like a believer, not a skeptic. How could he not? Afterall, he was witnessing a confrontation between a person possessed and a person under mind control by an extra-terrestrial. It was time to look at the evidence laid out in front of him.

They were real.

Basil had no time to focus on the epiphany. Meshy was out of the game and this show needed a host. He stepped in front of the camera.

"I can't believe I'm saying this. Our investigation into the haunted Hamburger House has revealed not only the presence of paranormal energy but extra-terrestrial activity as well. As you can see, over my shoulder, two of our team members are being controlled by supernatural forces. A third, our psychic, Paloma is currently in a static state, the apparent vessel of an energy exchange taking place between the ghosts and the alien."

Bucky panned the camera from Basil to a frozen, glowing Paloma, then zoomed the camera past Basil and focused in on the action.

48

Ko GOT HIS GROOVE BACK. He wasn't as strong as even one half of Crumbles. He wasn't cut out for the spirit realm. He wanted to go home and find peace at last. It sucked being the victim of a murder. So much unfinished business.

He was stuck to his fryolator. A bond strengthened by his murder and his connection to the place. Classic ghost stuff. Find an object with a sordid history and you are sure to find a spirit bound to it. Chances are, that spirit will be none too happy about being trapped. Spirits that were bound to objects or places were neither here, nor there. They were between.

Ko was between and ready to go home. The problem was, he never saw who murdered him. That's what got him stuck. The police never solved the murder. Sure, everyone speculated it was the clown, Crumbles, but speculation and reality never make good bedfellows.

Bottom line: Crumbles didn't do it. He was set up. Ko didn't have to see his killer to know that fact. Crumbles wasn't a murderer. That clown loved Hamburger House too much to taint its reputation as anything less than a wholesome family establishment.

Murder? In Hamburger House? No way. Nobody understood that. Nobody knew Crumbles better than Ko.

Ko would stick by Crumbles to the end. They were past the end and Ko was still as loyal as ever to his co-worker and compatriot.

Now, he faced murder a second time. The energy drain. He and Crumbles were the power source of Hamburger House. They and the building were the same being. It was hard to describe in terms the living could comprehend. Ko felt the compulsion to cook, like he did when he was alive. And the equipment would come to life. But, more like he and his fryolator were one and they came to life together to do what they did. It was a cycle that would happen over and over again until...

Resolution?

Ko assumed it would take the resolution of his murder to break free and find peace. He'd waited so long. The murderer must be dead by now, never to be exposed for his crime. Ko, never to receive vindication for his death. No resolution, ever.

Maybe it would be best if he allowed the others to take the energy from Hamburger House after all. How much worse could dying a second time be to an eternity bound to a fryolator? Maybe, a second death would bring nothingness. Sweet, merciful nothingness.

Ko knew that would be selfish. If he went, so did Crumbles and Crumbles wasn't ready to go. He'd have to help. Perhaps if Crumbles could inhabit the living, so could Ko?

And here was a perfectly fine woman, standing in the lobby going to waste. He moved to her. A ball of condensed energy was bound within her space. Ko worried about tapping into that much raw energy. He was so weak though, perhaps it couldn't hurt?

He stepped into the one they called Paloma and came to life.

49

KO FOUND ALL of his stolen energy within Paloma.

"Hi, nice to meet you." Ko said and Paloma spoke.

Possession was a new skill Paloma discovered. She wasn't used to it at all. Channeling a spirit was one thing, but this possession stuff was wild. With channeling, she could hear the spirits whispering to her from somewhere, everywhere and nowhere. Possession was odd, she lost control to one degree or another. With the clown, it was like she was shoved into the background somewhere, forced to watch herself like a child punished in a corner.

This time, Paloma felt something between possession and channeling. There was a spirit there, she knew because it made her speak. Or, to be more precise, it spoke to her from within and thus influenced her to speak the words the spirit intended. Regardless, she still had her full faculties.

"Hello, spirit. Who are you?" Paloma asked aloud.

"Oh cool, you can hear me. I'm Ko. I'm on fries." Ko spoke aloud through and to Paloma.

"Have you been turning the fryolator on and off all day? Are you the energy that flows through Hamburger House?" Paloma asked Ko aloud.

"Yes. That's me. Not all of it. Mostly just my fryolator. I died there you know? But also, Crumbles is here. His energy is stronger. But, it's weaker now. You have a lot of our energy here. I can see it within you. Do you think we could have it back? I'm feeling awfully weak and I'm afraid I won't last."

Paloma gasped. She was the energy vessel. She was supposed to bring it to Thwrp. She was cut off. It all came rushing back. The spirits must have cut off her connection to Thwrp. They had to be responsible. She was killing them.

She felt awful.

"I did not realize I was doing that to you. There is a being that needs your energy or he will die," Paloma spoke aloud.

"Crumbles will not allow that." Ko spoke through Paloma, "He needs to become one again. The alien is trying to kill us. Don't you understand?"

Paloma understood everything now. Crumble's spirit was split. Outside, his spirit was in its happy place. Inside, it was tortured. An unreconciled soul. Amazing. It made sense.

She spoke aloud to Ko, "We must help Crumbles. The alien can't have your energy."

Paloma felt what Ko felt, conflict. "But the alien will die. You said that yourself."

"But you will die if he takes all your energy."

"I think there's enough for everyone. The two Crumbles must come together."

"What. The. Fuck?" Paloma heard Bucky say.

She turned. Both she and Ko saw Bucky, pie-eyed with his camera trained on them.

He'd captured Paloma speaking to herself.

"How'd you do that?"

Paloma cast her open palms toward Bucky like she was a witch casting a spell. White tendrils of smoke wisped from her hands and encircled Bucky. His eyes rolled into the back of his head.

"We got him!" Ko said through Paloma.

"Cool trick!" Bucky said in Paloma's mind.

Ko had reeled Bucky under his sway. They operated as a triad now. Even better, in her mind's eye, she could see through the viewfinder of Bucky's camera. With ghost energy in their corner, they were able to use the camera's electromagnetic ability to see what ghosts saw. The Ko-Paloma-Bucky trio had spectral vision.

And they could see the two Crumbles clear as day.

50

NUMBER A HADN'T WOKEN up that morning expecting to see an alien. He took the job at the Intergalactic League of Inter-Galaxies & Collectibles because he couldn't get hired anywhere else. He'd been run ragged through a series of retail management positions, each a bigger nightmare than the one before it. The last straw had been the shoe store.

He found the want ad for the position at the ILIG&C stapled to a telephone pole up the street from his basement apartment.

WANTED: Responsible person to oversee Southwestern Division Field Office of the Intergalactic League of Inter-Galaxies and Collectibles. Rigid hours, slightly competitive wages and a benefits package sans dental, medical and 401k. Prior experience in retail gift shop management is a plus. All travel paid for on occasion. Contact Mobius 6-5000.

The position didn't sound like a retail job even though they were looking for retail experience. Number A thought maybe it was a comic book distribution house or something to that effect. Besides, he did a short stint as the overnight manager of a souvenir shop near a lake resort just outside of Santa Fe back in the early 90s. You never knew retail management hell until you dealt with New

Mexican lake resort tourists at two o'clock in the morning. Those people were demonic.

The want ad had not mentioned aliens. Number A soon found out in training that part of the job would be scouting and tracking "Intergalactic persons of interest" as the training manager put it. The core of the drilling, however, involved procurement of trinkets, oddities, curiosities, tchotchkes and various bric-a-brac. In other words, collectibles.

Number A rose through the ranks of the Southwestern Branch of the ILIG&C. He'd been told by his various supervisors over the years that his procurements were some of the biggest selling collectibles not only in the division but in the whole of the US Regional District of the ILIG&C.

All that was great until today. This morning, he was asked, for the first time in his tenure at ILIG&C to scout and track an intergalactic person of interest. He was to take his protege, Number B with him, sit in a van and be on the lookout for "a sickly meat-colored Thwrpian." Their directive indicated a rival scouting team, outfitted with a psychic, could lead them to their target.

All intelligence pointed to an old, roadside hamburger joint just outside of San Jon. Hamburger House.

Until Number A floated in front of the sickly meat colored Thwrpian, he had no idea what one even looked like. He dared not let Number B know his ignorance of the facts. He was Number B's superior after all.

But this was as new to him as it was to Number B. In fact, it never dawned on him that the term 'intergalactic persons of interest' meant freakin' aliens!

Number A was forced to come to the realization that his one and only successful long-term career was finding crap for aliens to buy and take back to their homes.

Even though he and his partner were now held captive by the sickly meat-colored alien, he would have to call this job a success. They *had* tracked and scouted the intergalactic person of interest, on his first try no less!

There was no directive nor training on how to proceed once the alien was found. Maybe he was supposed to upsell him on some low-cost, high-margin beach towels? The directive folder from the ILIG&C was back in the van.

Number A was stuck. He was going to eat shit at the office if this job got botched. Number B was sure to get promoted, somehow, someway. It wasn't fair. He wished he could just zoom off with the alien. That would be easiest. Escape it all.

Number A didn't understand any of what was going on. There was an argument. The sickly, meat-colored alien was arguing with one of the women. The woman seemed possessed, like the psychic had been when they attempted to abduct her.

Ghosts and aliens. All real.

Number A wondered if ghosts were into collectibles as well. Who was he kidding? He wasn't cut out for this line of work anymore. He wanted to go back to being Steve Ehrsloug. That's who he was before he became Number A, a nameless employee.

51

"GIVE ME MY ENERGY!" Thwrp demanded through Meshy.

"Get outta my way!" Crumbles insisted through Addy.

Meshy shoved Addy. Addy shoved Meshy. Neither one budged.

"Here," Paloma offered a paper cup between the two supernatural forces.

The red and white striped cup was filled with a blue aura. The same cup Ko used to scooped piping hot, salted French fries in, now contained something the irate customers desired even more. Energy.

"Fuel!" Meshy exclaimed. It was Thwrp who was excited.

Paloma spoke, "I can get you more, but you must allow my friend to step by you."

Meshy snagged the cup from Paloma's hand.

"Meshy." Paloma said, not Ko, "I know the alien Thwrp has your mind. Let him know it's okay. The ghosts are not harmful. They can help if Thwrp will let them. If he takes all the energy however, he'll kill our ghosts. We'll lose the story. There will be nothing left to haunt Hamburger House."

Meshy heard Paloma from the back corner of his mind. He

called Thwrp. It would be okay. They could help him. The ghosts were his friends. Meshy was his friend. Let the ghost past.

Thwrp understood. Plus, the cup that held the energy would get his vessel started. The fact that it came in a nifty souvenir cup was a bonus.

Meshy stepped aside. Addy walked past. She stopped and looked Thwrp in the eyes, and nodded, they were okay.

Addy continued outside. She strode to the side of Route 66, still walking like she wore clown shoes. She was able to see Happy Crumbles. But it wasn't Addy that saw him, it was Angry Crumbles.

Now that he stepped outside and was approaching the place that made his job so much fun, he was beginning to feel a lot less angry about everything that had happened. He knew now why this part of him stayed out here. Out here there was hope coming down the road at any moment, if he just waited long enough.

Inside he was pent up with his anger. Locked away with his emotions, letting them fester behind closed doors. He was ready to be whole again.

His happy half turned away from the road, waiting to wave at passing vehicles. The balloon he held perked up. The happy Crumbles nodded at him. The angry Crumbles nodded back.

They reached out and hugged one another.

Addy was ejected from their space. She fell back onto the dusty gravel and looked up. She saw Crumbles, spectral like an angel. He was spectacular.

52

EVERYONE COULD SEE the ghost of Crumbles the Clown. He invited everyone inside Hamburger House for a bite to eat and a chance to rest on their long journey.

Everyone obliged, even Thwrp.

Crumbles led the group inside. When he walked in the lobby, all the lights came on. Ko lit up as well and looked as spectacular as Crumbles. Ko smiled and waved to Crumbles and their guests. He took up his station at the fryolator and fired it up.

Addy wasn't freaked out. This place *was* haunted. It was haunted to the nines. The ghosts that haunted Hamburger House were nice. With the help of Meshy and his team, they'd been able to make their peace.

Crumbles led everyone to the front counter. He walked around the other side and asked what they'd like to have.

"Burgers and fries for everyone!" Addy said and giggled.

Thwrp, still talking through Meshy said, "I'll pass on the burr gurr and frize. I will take a super-sized order of energy. And your finest collectible. To go."

"Energy!" Crumbles exclaimed, "Of course! I've got lots of energy for you my little friend. Let's get your ship fueled up and get you on your way! Where are you headed? Vegas? Los Angeles? Maybe taking the kids to Disneyland?"

"Nah, I'm headed to Thwrp." Thwrp said through Meshy.

Crumbles face lit up, "Oh! I hear it's lovely there this time of year. Ok then, let's get you on your way."

While Ko cooked up burgers and fries for everyone, Crumbles opened the back door and tapped his red clown nose. A beam of energy flowed out of his nostrils and curled through the air to Thwrp's dumpster shaped spacecraft.

The energy beam connected with the ship and the craft's engine roared to life like a muscle car.

Everyone cheered.

"Okay, I'll be going now." Thwrp said through Meshy.

"Wait," Crumbles said, "don't forget your souvenir."

Crumbles fished a flaccid red balloon out of his pocket and gave it a few stretches. He put it to his lips and it expanded into a long hot dog. Crumbles nodded and smiled at everyone. He began twisting and folding the balloon, sculpting it into a shape. Everyone was eager to see what he was crafting.

He held it out when completed. It was a clown face. He offered it to Thwrp.

Thwrp took it, "This is the finest collectible I've ever been given in this entire galaxy."

Meshy carried Thwrp to his ship. He lifted the alien off his back and placed him inside.

Thwrp broke the connection with Meshy, and set down the two guys from the desert.

"Wait! Take me with you! There's nothing left for me here," Number A begged.

"You're going to leave me here?" Number B asked Number A.

Number A put a reassuring hand on Number B's shoulder, "You've got this. I've taught you everything I know. You're ready. They like you back at the office. You'll be going places. Me, I'm too old to fight my way up the corporate ladder any more. There's nothing left for me to do here. The only way I'm going up in this world is to get in that spaceship and ride it to the heavens."

Number B nodded, "I'm gonna miss you."

Thwrp said, *"Murrble nurrble glrrble blrrt."*

"Shotgun!" Number A yelled and hopped in the dumpster next to Thwrp.

The lid closed and the ship rose into the clear New Mexican night. It shot straight up and was soon just a pin prick of light like every other celestial body in the sky.

53

THIS PLACE IS HAUNTED!
  This place is haunted!
  This place is haunted!

Addy said it to herself over and over again as she counted the days intake at Haunted Hamburger House (and Collectibles.)

Haunted Hamburger House was a bona fide hit. They'd opened up the business not long after Thwrp blasted off into the cosmos with the mysterious Number A in tow. The business brought back significant traffic flow along their stretch of Route 66. Haunted Hamburger House wasn't the only establishment prospering either. All around them, businesses popped up to support the new influx of visitors. There were ghost-themed gas stations, alien-inspired convenience stores, paranormal restaurants, motels haunted by paid actors and, of course, a souvenir shop loaded with cheap intergalactic goodies (all made in China).

Basil put together their business plan. Serve quality, fresh hamburgers at a premium price. They could get top dollar for classic American cuisine since it was being cooked up by legitimate ghosts. The proof was irrefutable since Meshy's ghost investigations show aired on TV.

Not Normal Investigations was the first ever ghost hunting show on television to capture actual footage of paranormal activity. Meshy and Paloma became overnight superstars. Already, they were contracted for a second and third season of their runaway hit paranormal investigation show, Not Normal Investigations. They also were signed on for a spin-off show focused on the search for extraterrestrial life.

Bucky wasn't the cameraman any more. Not since he proposed to Addy and started working the register at Haunted Hamburger House. He and Addy had set the date for the wedding in the fall. They hired Meshy's new cameraman, Number B, to film the ceremony.

Number B quit the agency after they gave him a promotion. He learned about the agency's failure to comply with intergalactic policies and procedures, highlighted by a series of complaints lodged against them from a source from the planet Thwrp. He couldn't continue to work for a hapless outfit. Meshy hired him on the spot. Number B was a great fit. He never put the camera down.

Outside Haunted Hamburger House, Crumbles continued to welcome the crowds. The only difference this time was that they weren't on their way to Vegas or The Grand Canyon or Napa Valley. They were on a road trip to visit Haunted Hamburger House. They came to see Crumbles, the happy ghost clown.

And they could see him. He was pure energy. A true-to-life-ghost just like everyone saw on TV. He was a celebrity too. The line to get a complimentary collectible clown face balloon from Crumbles was as long as the line to get inside and get a juicy cheeseburger and ghost fried French fries, cooked up steaming hot by Ko.

Addy stuffed the stacks of bills into the deposit bag. She smiled. She was so happy this place was haunted.

The End

FRANK J. EDLER

Frank J. Edler is the author of many twisted novels and uncanny short stories often cited as 'laugh out loud' reads. His work walks the fine line between horror and the bizarre. He resides in New Jersey, a land that is both horrific and bizarre. When not writing, Mr. Frank hosts the wildly popular *Bizzong! The Weird & Wacky Fiction Podcast* heard exclusively on Project Entertainment Network.

Other Books by Frank J. Edler
   Death Gets a Book
   Brats in Hell
   Scatterbrain
   Catcoin: The Fictional History of a Cryptocurrency
   A Death in Toledo
   Exploding Bears: A Savage Comedy
   Scared Silly
   Uncomfortable Shorts

   With Armand Rosamilia

Shocker
   Shocker II: Love Gun
   Shocker III: Slippery When Wet

   With Chuck Buda, Tim Meyer and Armand Rosamilia
   Beers and Fears: The Haunted Brewery

Beers and Fears: Flight Night

His social media contacts are:
    Facebook: www.facebook.com/FrankJEdler
    Twitter: @NJMetal
    Instagram: NJMetal
    Blog: frankjedler.blogspot.com
    TikTok: MrFrank732

ABOUT THE EDITOR / PUBLISHER

Dawn Shea is an author and half of the publishing team over at D&T Publishing. She lives with her family in Mississippi. Always an avid horror lover, she has moved forward with her dreams of writing and publishing those things she loves so much.

D&T Previously published material:
 ABC's of Terror
 After the Kool-Aid is Gone

Follow her author page on Amazon for all publications she is featured in.
 Follow D&T Publishing at the following locations:
 Website
 Facebook: Page / Group
 Or email us here: dandtpublishing20@gmail.com

-- 1st ed.

Haunted Hamburger House by Frank J. Edler

Edited by Tim and Dawn Shea

Cover by Anderson Leao

HAUNTED HAMBURGER HOUSE